CECILY LOOKED SUPERIOR AS GEORGE BEGAN TO RECITE . . .

Cecily's mouth dropped. George's piercing stare caught her eyes and held them. ". . . *It is my lady; O, it is my love! O, that she knew she were!*"

Cecily began to blush under George's unfaltering gaze. Her hand went to her hot cheek but she was unable to tear her eyes away. She sat mesmerized as he continued.

". . . *O, that I were a glove upon that hand, that I might touch that cheek!*" When George stopped the room was filled with silence—then the sound of clapping and enthusiastic praise.

George continued to look at Cecily, who lowered her eyes demurely and blushed.

"A country bumpkin, is it?" whispered her friend. "Country bumpkin, indeed!"

Faint Heart

Sheila Rabe

CHARTER/DIAMOND BOOKS, NEW YORK

FAINT HEART

A Charter/Diamond Book / published by arrangement with the author

PRINTING HISTORY
Charter/Diamond edition / December 1990

ISBN: 1-55773-427-5

Charter/Diamond Books are published by The Berkley Publishing Group, 200 Madison Avenue, New York, New York 10016.

PRINTED IN THE UNITED STATES OF AMERICA

10 9 8 7 6 5 4 3 2 1

For Robert.
Thanks again.

• 1 •

THE BEAUTIFUL LADY Wallingford sat in her elegant town house drawing room, the recipient of a letter informing her that her cousin was coming to the metropolis. "Your uncle says it is high time George got some town polish," wrote Aunt Agatha, "but I confess it quite terrifies me to think of my dear boy on his own in London. I would be so grateful, my dear Adriana, if you and your charming husband would take him under your wing and see that he stays out of trouble. He is an intelligent boy, but far too trusting, and I fear that some coming young miss might entrap him."

Adriana smiled at this, and her blue eyes took on a definite twinkle. She shook her head. Dear Aunt Agatha, she thought. George was a darling, but he was hardly the sort of young man who would attract a brazen young female looking for a good catch. He would inherit her father's estate as well as his own but that was certainly no fortune. And a young man who was heir only to a baronetcy could hardly hope to compete with an earl or a duke or even a viscount when it came to attracting the notice of scheming young ladies. Of course, if Cousin George was as handsome as her husband, Gerald, then Aunt would possibly have something to worry about. But, while George was nearly as tall as Lord Wallingford, he lacked his lordship's mature build. Cousin George merely was a passably nice-looking young man who had yet to grow into his lanky form. He was possessed of an amazing lack of address caused by chronic shyness, and only those who knew him well could appreciate him for the kind soul he was. In short, Cousin George, though cherished by his family, was hardly the sort of young man to take London by storm.

Adriana sighed and brushed her chin lightly with the fine stationery, lost in thought.

"Pondering a love note?" came a voice from the doorway.

Adriana jumped. "Gerald! You gave me a start," she scolded.

Gerald Shavely, the third Earl of Wallingford, sauntered into the room and settled himself next to his wife. "Should I have had Hastings announce me?" he asked with a grin.

"Yes," answered his wife. "I might have been entertaining a gentleman and would have liked some warning of your approach."

"You saucy thing!" declared Wallingford, leaning over and lifting his wife onto his lap.

Adriana struggled to free herself. "Gerald, the servants—"

"—Know very well how I feel about you. And after two years of seeing us together have probably gotten used to our odd behavior," finished her husband, nibbling her neck.

"Now that is quite enough," she said, leaving his lap and straightening her golden curls. "Aren't you even curious about this letter?"

"If you wish it I am curious."

"It is from Aunt Agatha."

"We are highly honored," murmured Wallingford.

"We are to have a visitor," Adrianna continued, ignoring this impertinence. "Cousin George will soon be visiting London and Aunt asks that we keep an eye on him and save him from any designing young women."

"Cousin George? You mean the scrawny scarecrow with the stumbling feet?" Wallingford burst out laughing. "Oh, yes," he said finally, wiping his eyes. "We shall guard him with our lives although we shall most likely have to save him from half the girls in town."

"You are being most unkind," said Adriana, forgetting her own private reaction not fifteen minutes earlier. "Cousin George is a dear."

"Yes," admitted Wallingford. "He's a good sort. But I doubt we shall have to worry about protecting him from scheming females. Thank God your aunt did not ask us to find one for him."

"A girl would have to look far to find a better man than my cousin."

"Yes, when it comes right down to it, you are right." agreed Wallingford. "I have it!" He clapped his hands together. "Let's engage him to my cousin Cecily and we will be done with both of them before the Season is even over."

Adriana was unamused and scolded her lord with a shake of the head. "Surely you would not wish a fate like that upon my cousin."

"There is nothing wrong with Cecily that won't disappear with time and a little less spoiling. You know how it is with famous beauties."

"I was a famous beauty myself not long ago," Adriana reminded him, "and I certainly never put on such airs."

"But you were not an only child whose destiny was to achieve the brilliant match your mama always dreamed of for herself."

Adriana sighed. "Yes, it is a shame. Cecily's mama has lived for this moment for years. I suppose that is what has made the child so spoiled. She has been given such a good opinion of herself for so long she has come to believe it. And she has such very high expectations, not to mention a high spirit. Goodness, but I never dreamed being a chaperon would be so difficult!"

"Yes, you looked positively careworn at my sister's ball last night," said her husband, lips quivering.

"Oh, pooh!" declared Adriana. "You cannot expect me to watch her every second, Gerald."

"No." Wallingford chuckled. "I think my aunt should be grateful we have taken her at all. I call it a dashed dirty trick to saddle a man with a houseguest when he's barely been married two years. Where, by the way, is she?"

"Still abed."

"I wish we were," said Wallingford, looking meaningfully at his wife.

Adriana blushed. "You are positively indecent. Anyway, I shan't go back now. I am up for the day."

"Mayhap I can change your mind," whispered her husband, edging closer to her.

Wallingford was never able to discover whether or not he would have been able to change his lady's mind. The door opened and a dainty, raven-haired beauty with thick lashed eyes and a perfect rosebud mouth entered the room.

Wallingford sank back in defeat on his side of the sofa and Adriana, trying to sound nonchalant, greeted the newcomer. "Hello, Cecily. How did you sleep?"

"Quite well, thank you," said Cecily.

"Have you breakfasted?"

Cecily nodded. "What shall we do today, Cousin?"

Adriana sighed inwardly. She had hoped to talk Gerald into taking her for a drive. In fact, if Cecily hadn't interrupted them . . . Well, one must be a good hostess. "What would you like to do?"

"I should like to go shopping. Sir Winston told me last night that deep blue would set off the highlights in my hair much better than pale blue, and I wish to have a ball gown made in that color."

Adriana mentally cursed Sir Winston for his sartorial advice. "I suppose we could go and look," she said noncommitally.

"Sir Winston said my hair actually shines blue, like a raven's wing when it catches the light," Cecily continued, going to the drawing-room mirror and turning her head from side to side. "I cannot tell myself. Do you think it does?"

Wallingford rolled his eyes in disgust.

"If Sir Winston says so it must be true," replied Adriana. "However, I have found that a deep blue ages one terribly. It's so . . . matronly." She wrinkled her nose in disgust for affect.

"Oh, that is only because it is not done by girls who are just out. But the Season is half over by now, and I am sure no one cares anymore about what color ball gown a girl wears. And besides, I think I would create a sensation in a dark blue ball gown."

"I am sure you would," agreed Adriana.

Cecily eyed her suspiciously, looking for evidence of hidden sarcasm in her remark, but her cousin-in-law merely smiled sweetly back at her. "Do you really think it would make me look old?" Cecily finally ventured.

Adriana shrugged. "Oh, probably not. I spoke without thinking. Pray, do not consider it."

Cecily stood silently before the mirror. "What do you think of a ball gown in pale blue?"

"The contrast between your dark hair and a pale blue gown would be most striking."

"Yes, I think so too," agreed Cecily, and Wallingford put a hand to his mouth to cover a smile. He saluted his wife on her clever management of his cousin with a wink.

Meanwhile, belowstairs Hastings was admitting a tall, young gentleman clad in a most handsome pair of biscuit-colored walking breeches which showed legs still in need of developing. His jacket, though well made, did little to disguise the fact that his chest also stood in need of the same. But his face was handsome enough, housing a finely chiseled nose and a pair of eyes almost too fine to be wasted on a male. His mouth was wide and his chin showed character. With a little more meat on his bones, thought Hastings, the young gentleman would be right handsome. But until time should take care of that particular problem the fellow definitely needed more padding in his jacket.

"Is my cousin at home?" inquired the new arrival.

"If you would care to follow me . . ." Hastings led the visitor upstairs and had just stopped in front of the drawing-room door when the young man put a restraining hand on his arm.

Fingers to his lips, he motioned for silence and whispered, "I want to surprise her."

Before Hastings could protest, the new arrival threw open the door and, with a grand gesture, entered the room. This alone would have been enough to catch the attention of its occupants, but before they could draw their breath he further amazed them by catching the toe of his boot on the carpet and pitching headlong into the room. He tried to right himself, but gravity won the day, and he landed in a heap on the floor, taking a nearby table and several expensive knickknacks with him.

Cecily stood openmouthed and gawking while Adriana let out a squeak and flew from the sofa to the young man's side.

Wallingford alone remained clam. "Cousin George," he said, "nice to see you again."

• 2 •

A BLUSHING GEORGE scrambled to his feet, trying simultaneously to set the overturned table and himself to rights.

"Oh, George, never mind the table!" exclaimed Adriana. "Are you hurt?" Without thinking she began to fix his cravat, causing him to turn yet a deeper shade of red.

"I am quite all right, really. I daresay all this was once valuable," George said, looking remorsefully at the broken china at his feet.

"There was nothing of importance there," lied Adriana. "Why, now that I think of it I cannot even remember what I had sitting on that table."

"I can," said Cecily helpfully. "Cousin Gerald just gave you that little—"

"Easily replaced," interrupted Wallingford. "George, I suppose I must introduce you to my cousin, Miss Cecily Hammond. This is Adriana's cousin, the honorable Mr. George Atherby."

"How do you do?" murmured Cecily.

George stood silent, obviously awed by what he saw. His cousin dug a subtle elbow into his side. "Oh, yes. How do you do?" he replied.

"Fine, thank you."

"That's nice," said George. As he took a step closer to the vision in the striped silk morning gown the broken figurines crunched under his foot, causing George's face to once again assume an unnaturally red hue.

"Do sit down, George," suggested Adriana, tugging the bellpull.

George subsided into a seat.

"When did you get to town?" his cousin asked.

"Yes," answered George, grinning at Cecily.

"*When* did you arrive, dearest?" Adriana repeated.

"Oh! I arrived yesterday."

Adriana waited for him to elucidate but as George seemed disinclined to do so she pumped him further. "Where are you staying? Have you found lodgings? . . . *George!*"

George pulled his attention away from the beauty seated across from him with an effort. "Beg pardon. What were you saying?"

"Have you found lodgings?"

"Yes. In Jermyn Street. I have just moved in."

"Wonderful!" declared Adriana. "It will be such fun having you in town. You shall, of course, have to dine with us next Wednesday and accompany us to Almack's."

"Do you go also, Miss Hammond?" inquired George hopefully.

Cecily's large violet eyes opened wide. "Why, of course. Anyone of any consequence must be seen at Almack's."

George blushed again, this time for his ignorance. "Of course," he murmured.

"In the meantime, perhaps you might like to accompany me to my tailor," suggested Wallingford.

"That's a devilish fine coat," admitted George, admiring not only the dark blue coat of bath superfine, but also the powerful torso it so perfectly covered. "Who is your tailor?"

"Weston," said Wallingford.

George's eyes widened. "Weston! I should say I would like to come with you!"

Wallingford smiled at his wife. "I daresay we can have

you looking as fine as five pence by next week," he assured George.

George smiled and took a glass from the tray with which Hastings had magically appeared. He was going to have a coat made by Weston and he was going to Almack's with the most beautiful girl in the world. Cecily favored him with a polite smile and he grinned back. His cup ran over, figuratively and, unfortunately, literally.

"Really!" exclaimed Cecily later as she and her chaperon set out on their shopping expedition. "I have never seen anyone so provincial—or so clumsy. I thought I should die of laughter when your cousin spilled his wine. No one would ever guess he is related to you."

Adriana frowned. To hear her favorite cousin talked of in such terms did not please her, and she sprang to his defense. "I admit Cousin George lacks town polish but he is a dear, sweet fellow, and lots of fun. A girl could do much worse than to fall in love with George."

"I don't know about that," countered Cecily, "but I do know a girl could do much better. And I certainly intend to. Why, what would Mama say if I were to throw myself away on a mere nobody."

Adriana could think of a few things to say as to who would be thrown away on whom but she held her tongue. After all, Cecily was spoiled and thoughtless, but there was really no meanness in her. Still, Adriana couldn't help hoping George would find another young lady attractive when they visited Almack's the next week.

George himself, however, had no such desire. He left his cousin's town house determined to impress Miss Cecily Hammond and make her believe he was a man of the world, not some ignorant fellow just arrived from the country.

Of course, George was nothing if not honest, and he realized that an ignorant fellow from the country was exactly what he was. His parents had been happy to leave the London whirl behind and, with the exception of schooling, their son had been little exposed to the rigors of town life. But he was eager to learn. He longed to become familiar with all the haunts of the fashionable young bloods and was ready to become an intimate of Brooks's and Boodle's, as well as Jackson's boxing salon. He also had a desire to visit Cribb's Parlour and drink White Lightning and intended to have a look in at Tattersall's as soon as possible.

And while he visited Hoby and Weston and all the other establishments that existed to keep the ton looking superior, he cherished a vision of himself transformed into a godlike creature with powerful thighs and a massive chest. His vision naturally included the beautiful Miss Hammond, staring raptly up into his face.

The following week George arrived at the Wallingford's town house looking very natty in his evening attire. His shoulders and chest still did not appear massive, but they at least looked passable, thanks to some clever padding on Mr. Weston's part. And his calfs, while still not shapely, at least looked elegant in his new silk stockings.

Wallingford ushered him into the library and George, who had been feeling quite dashing and pleased with his new look, couldn't help comparing himself to his host. He gazed at the earl's square, strong shoulders and sighed.

As if sensing his guest needed some bolstering up, Wallingford offered him an encouraging smile along with a glass of Madeira and said, "You're looking good tonight, George. I daresay you will have to fight the ladies away."

George smiled and shook his head. "Doing it a bit too brown, Cousin. I feel like a scarecrow next to you."

"Well, you don't look it," replied Wallingford.

George opened his mouth as if to say something, then

shut it again determinedly. This action wasn't lost on his host. "You know, George, since you're going to be in town for a while you might like to visit Jackson's with me. I've gone a few with the Gentleman himself, and I think you might enjoy putting the gloves on. I have found that a good workout does wonders for the chest and shoulders."

"Really?" said George, eyes brightening with a new vision of himself. George had longed to visit the famous establishment at number 13 Bond Street, where the man known as the emperor of pugilism held court. With Wallingford's words, longing turned to determination.

"Come by tomorrow and I will take you round," promised Wallingford. "That is, if you still have the energy. An evening of tedium at Almack's can be very taxing."

George could not imagine his evening being tedious if spent in the company of the vision that floated into the room as Wallingford was speaking. Cecily was wearing a pale pink gown hemmed with multiple flounces. Her dark hair was dressed a la Titus, parted in the center and allowed to fall in charmingly disheveled curls. "Good evening," she murmured, holding out a tiny hand encased in white kid.

George took it and once possessed of it showed no inclination to let go. Cecily blushed and finally yanked her hand free, causing George to curse himself silently.

"We are ready so there is no sense in delaying your fate any longer, gentlemen," said Adriana lightly, trying to ease an awkward moment.

"Yes, well, let us be on our way," said Wallingford with an overabundance of heartiness. They followed George and Cecily out of the library. "If things continue like this the evening promises to be a disaster," Wallingford whispered to his lady.

Adriana merely gave him a quelling look and sailed down the front steps and out to the waiting carriage.

As usual Almack's was crowded with the elite of London society. Young men stood in groups eyeing the debutantes who were decked out in ruffled and ribboned gowns of various pastel shades and accompanied by watchful mamas. Older and married women, no longer required to wear the same properly demure colors of their younger sisters, added drama to the scene with their gowns of richer hues. Their jewels sparkled and their fans flirted, yet the majority of the people present wore expressions of haughty boredom. "How this institution remains when all our celebrated patronesses can offer us is lemonade and stale cake is more than I can fathom," grumbled Wallingford.

"You seemed to like it well enough three years ago," his wife reminded him.

"That is because I came to see you," he said, smiling down at her.

"Perhaps that is why Almack's still remains. The gentlemen still come to seek that certain lady. And I certainly hope George finds one here tonight," she added, watching her cousin.

Wallingford followed her gaze. George was standing on the edge of the crowd, watching Cecily and her dance partner with a jealous eye. "He is badly smitten, isn't he?"

"I am afraid so. Oh, Gerald, I have introduced him to no less than six eligible girls so far and not one of them interests him. What am I to do?"

"Find six more, I suppose," said Wallingford. "Though I doubt it will do you much good. I am afraid your cousin is destined to have his heart broken by my cousin. Perhaps you should let nature run its course. The sooner it happens, the sooner he will be able to pick up the pieces and find some other girl to interest him."

Adriana bit her lip. "I can think of a dozen girls who

would be better suited for him than Cecily. But if it is Cecily he wants then I shall have to help him get her."

"Stay a minute," said Wallingford, gently catching his wife's arm as she began to cross the room. "Let's not meddle. It can only cause problems."

"Gerald. You should know me better than that. I am not going to meddle. I am only going to help," replied Adriana, removing her husband's restraining hand.

Heaven help us all, thought Wallingford, as he watched his elegant wife make her way across the crowded room. Adriana had a talent for plunging into trouble, always with the best of motives. Poor Cousin George. Before his wife was done her cousin would definitely have had a memorable visit to London.

Unaware of the great adventure awaiting him, Cousin George stood transfixed, watching his goddess execute the intricate steps of the quadrille. He longed to be one of the lucky men to lead her onto the dance floor, but fear of disgracing himself kept him rooted where he stood. Also he feared that he would have no chance among the throng of suitors who vied for her attention.

"You really should ask her to dance," said a voice at his elbow.

George smiled at his cousin then returned his gaze to the dancers.

"Well?" she prompted.

"Hmmmmmm?"

"Are you going to ask her to dance?"

"There is no sense in even trying. She is besieged with suitors."

"Oh, come now. I have never seen you so fainthearted. This is not like you. You are every bit as worthy as any of those other men who are swarming around her."

George shook his head doubtfully.

"Come now, Cousin. Faint heart never won fair maiden. Look. The dance is ending. Go after her. Is she not worth fighting for?" George still hesitated. "If you do nothing some other man will carry her off under your very nose."

This final admonition had the desired effect. George set his jaw and strode purposefully across the room to where Cecily was holding court. He elbowed his way through the group of young men muttering, " 'Scuze me," and "Beg pardon," and finally reached her.

The last set of elegantly shoed toes he trampled belonged to a handsome young man as tall as himself, whose shoulders obviously owed their width to no one but his maker. Lord Spenser, the fourth Earl of Oswald, looked with some irritation at the clumsy intruder. "I say, you might watch where you are planting your feet, fellow," he snapped.

A slight blush betrayed Cecily's embarrassment. "Lord Spenser, this is the honorable George Atherby. He is Lady Wallingford's cousin and he is very clumsy, so I am sure he did not mean to step on your foot."

George begged his lordship's pardon. "I think I am still growing," he added by way of explanation.

"Good God, I should hope not," said a short, young man with a fat face and sandy blond hair, laughing. "How d'ye do? Name's Eagan. Are you an Eaton man? You look familiar."

"Yes, as a matter of fact, I am," said George with a smile, glad to meet a friendly face. The music started and George became suddenly inspired. "I daresay you may have forgotten you promised me this dance, Miss Hammond. I promise I shall be careful not to tread on your toes." He held out his hand expectantly.

It was obvious Cecily didn't wish to be parted from her company of admirers. She frowned but went with George.

"I do not remember promising you this dance," she said as they took their places for the next set.

"You didn't promise me any," admitted George. "But now that we are here we may as well, don't you think?"

Cecily smiled in spite of her irritation. "You are very impertinent," she said.

"I am very smitten," admitted George.

"Everyone who sees me is," said Cecily. "But really, you must not be, for I am convinced we would not suit and if I were to break your heart Cousin Adriana would be excessively unhappy with me."

"I promise I will not tell her if you break it, then you shan't have to worry."

"Now you are teasing," laughed Cecily.

George's blue eyes widened. "No. Why would I tease you?"

"I don't know," said Cecily. "But you look the type." After a moment's silence she conceded, "You really are a very fine dancer."

"Yes, I am, aren't I?" agreed George, pleased with himself.

"It is not very modest of you to agree," Cecily chided.

"I did no more than admit the truth. Surely that is no less modest than you admitting that you are beautiful."

"And pray, what might you mean by that remark, sir?" demanded Cecily.

"Why, nothing—" George began. Just at that moment Cecily's flounce became trapped under his foot. The noise of tearing fabric brought their attention instantly to their feet.

"Oh, look what you have done!" wailed Cecily.

George looked. So did their neighbors. He took her arm and escorted her off the floor and back to his cousin.

Lord Spenser, who had been jealously observing his

rival, smiled as he watched George lead a highly irritated Cecily from the floor. "Positively bucolic," he murmured to a friend. "He's her cousin, you say?"

His lordship's crony nodded. "Seems nice enough. Rather clumsy, though, ain't he?"

"Ah, well, we cannot all be light-footed," said Lord Spenser in the tone of one who knew that he did not fall into the same unfortunate category as Mr. Atherby.

"There will be the devil to pay for the poor fellow now," predicted his friend.

And indeed there was. "Your great oaf of a cousin has ruined my gown," Cecily declared.

"Oh, stuff!" exclaimed Adriana, examining the tear. "That is easily mended."

"A gown is never the same once it's mended," said Cecily disdainfully.

George sighed as she and Adriana disappeared to repair the ruined gown. This was not a good way to begin a courtship. But the Atherbys were not quitters. He would win the beautiful Miss Hammond or his name wasn't—

"I say old fellow," said the honorable Mr. Eagan, suddenly at his elbow. "Do you care for cockfighting? And, by the way, what did you say your name was?"

"The name," answered George with fierce determination, "is Atherby—George Atherby."

• 3 •

"I HOPE YOU gave her a sharp set down!" exclaimed Adriana's sister-in-law, Lady Elizabeth Raine, as the two women sat taking tea the next day in Lady Elizabeth's cozy drawing room.

"Most assuredly I did. Such uncharitable behavior. I left her home with strict instructions that if George should happen to call she is to apologize for her behavior and make amends to him. Else I shall wash my hands of her and send her home to her mama."

Elizabeth looked shocked. "But you are here," she protested.

"Give me some credit as a chaperon, I beg of you. I have left Gerald home to stand guard over her. I am quite out of patience with the girl and could not not abide the thought of her company this afternoon, which is why I have escaped here." Adriana sighed. "Really, I detest this job of chaperoning Cecily. I do not think I am at all cut out for it."

Elizabeth laughed. "Truer words were never spoken. But you married the head of the family and it is now your unfortunate lot to help every relative and hanger on, no matter how small the connection."

Adriana made a face.

"Don't despair, dearest. If the going gets too rough you know you may send her to us."

"Yes, but I wouldn't dream of afflicting you so. It is not

that Cecily is so very bad. The problem is we are too close in age. I am only three years older than she. It hardly puts me in a position of authority. The only way I can control her is to outsmart her."

"Surely you have no trouble doing that."

"Thus far I have managed well enough, but I will be greatly relieved when the Season is over. I must confess, it has not been as easy to handle Cecily as I thought it would be. She is so headstrong."

"How fortunate for you she is not imaginative as well," murmured Elizabeth with a smile.

"You may well laugh," said Adriana. "You do not have to produce a proper husband from her swarm of suitors."

"Do not despair," said Elizabeth. "There is always Sir Winston. His fortune is large enough to please even the most discriminating of mamas."

Adriana frowned. "I am sure Sir Winston is merely amusing himself by flirting with her. I doubt she will ever be able to bring him up to scratch. The only purpose he has served this Season has been to fill her head with all manner of foolish notions. His taste in clothes is impeccable and his advice perfect . . . for a mature woman. But for a girl just making her comeout . . ." Adriana shuddered. "If he wishes to have a hand in choosing her wardrobe he may offer for her. Otherwise, I do wish Sir Winston would confine himself to taking an interest in his mistress' clothing and quit filling Cecily's head with silly ideas."

Elizabeth giggled at her sister-in-law's mention of a subject to which well-bred ladies never referred except in moments of extreme asperity. "Perhaps he will surprise you and offer for her," she said.

Adriana shook her head. "You know as well as I that fat old toad has slipped through countless fingers these past ten years or more. Cecily will not be the first famous beauty who cast out lures to Sir Winston and wound up with nothing but a closetful of unsuitable gowns to show for her trouble."

Elizabeth shrugged as if to say stranger things have happened.

"I do wish her mama would have roused herself from her couch and come with Cecily," Adriana complained.

"Oh, but she suffers so," said Elizabeth in mock pity.

Adriana's blue eyes met her sister-in-law's brown ones and they exchanged knowing smiles. Adriana took a meditative sip of tea. "And now here is poor George besotted with her. Though after last night . . ." Adriana shook her head. "I do believe after last night if she and George were left alone Cecily would not be compromised—only murdered!"

At that very moment the honorable George Atherby stood on his cousin's doorstep, staring at the knocker. He twisted the posy he was carrying nervously. Now that he was here he heartily wished himself elsewhere. Yet no British soldier had ever faced the bayonets of Bonaparte's men with more determination than George showed the brass lion glaring at him. By sheer force of will he grabbed the ring that hung through its nose and slammed it against the door, all the while hoping the butler would tell him everyone was gone from home.

But Hastings had his orders. Her ladyship would be back soon and desired her cousin to wait. Would Mr. Atherby be so good as to follow him?

George obeyed and managed to enter the drawing room upright this time. Here he found the cause of his nervousness.

Cecily, for some unfathomable reason, looked almost as nervous as George, a fact which helped to put him a little more at ease. "My cousin will be joining us in just a few moments, but before he does I must apologize for my behavior last night," she said.

"No. It is I who must apologize," began George.

"Pray, do not," said Cecily. "Adriana fairly chewed my head off all the way home last night. I know I did not behave very prettily. Although I must say you were rather rude . . ." Cecily stopped herself. "But that is neither here nor there. I should not have made such a big fuss over so little a thing as a torn flounce. It was very stupid of me and I realize now I must have embarrassed you. I know I should not like to be embarrassed publicly and I am sorry, truly. It is just that you vexed me so," she finished.

George did not quite know what to say to all this. He stood silently, holding the flowers he had brought for her.

"Well, do not stand there staring at me as if I were some creature in the Zoological Garden," snapped Cecily, beginning to blush.

"Oh, beg pardon," stammered George.

"What have you there?" she asked.

"For you," replied George, offering the flowers. A petal fluttered to the ground.

Cecily's smile faded as she inspected George's offering. In his agitation he had treated the flowers rather carelessly, and they showed it.

George flushed and smiled weakly.

"The trouble is," Adriana was saying to her sister-in-law, "he is besotted with Cecily. So much so that he becomes absolutely tongue-tied around her."

"What? The fellow who took such an active part in our theatricals last Christmas, the one who nearly talked my ear off with his theories about modern farming methods? I can scarce credit it."

Adriana shook her head and sighed. "Thus far he has hardly showed himself to advantage. He seems doomed to suffer some new embarrassment whenever he is in Cecily's presence. Of course, she does nothing to help, for ever since his unfortunate first impression she sees him only as a buffoon and does not trouble to hide it. I would just as soon he find someone else," Adriana continued, helping herself to another tea cake, "but it's plain as a pikestaff he has his heart set on her. And since he wants her I think we should help him get her."

"We?"

"You do want to help, don't you?"

Elizabeth laughed. "I suppose I do. After all, George is your favorite cousin, and you are my dearest friend. If you must help him, I must help you. Besides, the Season has become sadly flat. Playing Cupid should prove to be quite diverting. How shall we go about this?"

"I think we might start with a small dinner party. Just the family and perhaps a few close friends—something where George can shine."

"That sounds harmless enough. Shall we have it here?"

"Gerald and I can as easily host it. But do come, and be thinking of what we can do to help show George off to advantage. Once she sees him at his best, Cecily cannot help but love him."

Adriana arrived home to find her cousin had already come and gone.

"I found him and Cecily enjoying an awkward silence," said Wallingford. "I believe he had given her slightly damaged flowers and was at a loss to explain how they had come to be so mauled. Your poor captive was very uncomfortable, so I took pity on him and set him free."

"Oh, dear," sighed Adriana, while untying her bonnet. "I am not at all sure they will suit."

"Nor I," agreed her husband. "So I hope you do not intend to continue playing the matchmaker." His wife was silent. "Adriana?" he said.

"Now, Gerald, what would you have me do? He is my cousin, after all."

"Yes, he is, and I should think you would have more regard for your cousin than to try and leg shackle him to mine."

"Cecily is not so bad," said Adriana, contradicting her earlier sentiments. "You said so yourself."

"Be that as it may, Cupid requires no help from you. And if he is going to unite your cousin and mine, you must allow him to strike in his own way and his own time."

"I shall," said Adriana. "But there is surely no harm in giving him the opportunity to work, at, say a small dinner party."

Wallingford cocked a reproving eyebrow at his lady, who stopped fussing with the feathers of her bonnet to give him a saucy look. "I suppose," he said, "you are determined upon this."

"Oh, Gerald, surely it is not meddling to throw a dinner party," said Adriana, casting aside her bonnet and laying imploring hands on her lord's chest. "I only want to give George the opportunity to shine," she continued, smoothing the fabric of his shirt. "And I know he would do so in the presence of his family, who love him."

"May I remind you he was in the presence of his family the first time he met my cousin?"

"Gerald!"

Wallingford sighed. "I know when I am beaten. Go ahead and throw your party, love. But do not pin too many hopes upon it. It has always been my observation that the more one tries to help Cupid, the more perverse pleasure he takes in foiling their efforts. He will shoot his arrows where he will, not where you wish."

"We shall see," replied Adriana. "I feel quite capable of taking on even Cupid himself, if that is what I must do for my cousin's sake."

"Well," said Wallingford, "after observing him today I should say he needs all the help he can get."

George definitely needed help dealing with the fairer sex (or at least one particular member of it). But in all other aspects of London social life he was soon faring quite well. The honorable Albert Eagan, future Viscount of Chetney, had taken a shine to him and called at his lodgings later that afternoon to find George moping about, rehashing his frustrating visit to Cecily.

"By Jove!" exclaimed Albert. "This is a stroke of luck. I am all alone for dinner tonight and badly in need of company. Why don't we toddle over to the club and have dinner? Then we can see some sport. Did you say you liked a good cockfight?"

George assured his new friend that he did and allowed himself to be led off for a night of strictly male companionship—a welcome change after a stressful afternoon spent dealing with female inconsistencies.

That was just the beginning. The honorable Albert Eagan and Mr. George Atherby became instant and fast friends, and between the efforts of Albert and Wallingford, George began to turn himself into a fashionable London buck. While Wallingford supervised the building of George's body and wardrobe, Albert took his social life firmly in hand, sponsoring him for membership in Brooks's club and showing him all the important sights of London, such as Astley's Amphitheatre, where George was properly impressed by the spectacle of what was billed as "grand military and equestrian melo-dramas" and a lady dancing bareback on a circus horse.

Of course, Astley's Amphitheatre was only the beginning. Albert also took his new friend to the opera, not to watch the performance of the popular Madame Pasta in Bellini's "Norma," but to see and be seen and to ogle the Cyprians installed in the boxes. Albert dragged a blushing George backstage to meet a pretty little dancer with a French accent, which Albert laughingly told George was about as French as his grandmother. A dainty girl with tiny, well-muscled legs, long, graceful arms, and an abundance of brown curls, the little dancer made George's pulse jump erratically. He regretfully left the theatre, wishing he was in plumper current and could afford a mistress.

Albert also added to George's circle of acquaintances by inviting him to a card party which left George with empty pockets, an aching head, and a wonderful feeling of belonging. Surely he was on his way to becoming a dashing man-about-town, the kind of man who could win a beautiful girl like Miss Cecily Hammond. Next time she saw him she would truly be amazed at the change in his appearance and manners, he told himself confidently.

• 4 •

THE PROSPECT OF a dinner party delighted both the principals involved, though for distinctly different reasons. Cecily was always ready for any kind of entertainment. She made a face when Adriana mentioned it was to be for her cousin George. But after a reproving look from her chaperon and a reminder of how nervous she had been when she first came to London, she shrugged her tiny shoulders and said, "Yes. Of course you are right. May we order ices from Gunter's?"

"We shall have to see if they received a shipment of ice from Greenland," replied Adriana, "but, if not, I thought we might order a sugar centerpiece."

Cecily clapped her hands. "Oh, yes—that would be capital! I shall enjoy your dinner party very much. And I promise I shall be nice to your cousin."

George could imagine nothing better than to be at a select dinner party with the girl of his dreams. With so few people present he was sure to have Cecily to himself. He accepted his cousin's invitation with alacrity.

Gilt-edged invitations were duly sent out to the other guests and, for the first time since her marriage to Wallingford, Adriana succeeded in keeping her small intimate party exactly that. Only a select few were honored. Of course, her sister and brother-in-law, Lord Raine and Lady Elizabeth Raine, were at the head of the guest list. George had requested that his new friend, the honorable Albert Eagan, be invited. And to make her numbers even Adriana had summoned Miss Catherine Courtland—Kate to her family and close friends. Miss Courtland was a young lady with auburn curls, large brown eyes and a sizable fortune to recommend her. Miss Courtland's curls weren't nearly as striking as Cecily's raven locks and her features weren't as perfect. Yet she was accounted a nice-looking young lady, and because of that and her sweet disposition she had many admirers. Her sweetness, combined with the fact that her beauty couldn't compete with Cecily's, made Cecily consider her a perfect friend, and Cecily was delighted to have her included in the party.

The day of the dinner party dawned bright and sunny—surely a good sign, George thought hopefully as he looked out his window. But what would he do to fill the long hours before the party? Jackson's! He would visit Jackson's. Why not do something with all this restlessness boiling inside him? George snatched up his new curly-brimmed beaver, set it on his head at a rakish angle, and ambled off down the street in the direction of number 13 Bond Street, feeling very much the man about town.

Cecily, too, was possessed of the energy brought on by anticipation, but she had to content herself by spending it helping her cousin with the last-minute arrangements and fussing over her toilet.

Half an hour before the party was to start the clouds which had been gathering since late afternoon burst, dropping a torrent of rain on the select streets of Mayfair. Cecily worried that perhaps such a downpour would keep the guests away, but it would take more than a cloudburst to keep members of the ton from fulfilling their social obligations. The fashionable hour of eight-thirty came and the guests began to arrive.

Lord Raine and his lady were the first at the door. Wallingford's tolerant smile as he bent down to allow Elizabeth a kiss on his cheek showed the affection he bore for his younger sister. The family resemblance was strong, showing especially around the nose and mouth. Elizabeth's coloring was not as dark as her brother's, but still dark enough to make a charming contrast to her husband's fairer complexion and light brown hair with its smattering of premature gray.

Raine clapped his brother-in-law on the back. "Hey ho. Only for you would we be about on such a night as even a duck would despise," he said to Adriana. "After seeing your cousin today I felt sure you would postpone the festivities."

"Why should I do that? Is George not feeling well?" asked Adriana.

Raine was prevented from answering by the entrance of Miss Catherine Courtland, followed by the Honorable Albert Eagan, who arrived only a few moments later. The new arrivals welcomed, Adriana was just about to question her brother-in-law further when Hastings announced her cousin. At the sight of him Adriana's mouth fell open. "George! What has happened to you?"

George blinked at his cousin with a swollen, purple eye lid. One side of his lip had grown grotesquely fat since she had last seen him. He made an attempt at a grin and winced. He would have been the picture of elegance in his black evening coat and black knee breeches, but his disfigured face took away from his fine dress, and the embarrassed blush he was now wearing added to his sorry appearance. "It's nothing much," he said, shrugging. "Markham got in a lucky hit."

Cecily wrinkled her nose in disgust. But Albert was

properly appreciative. "I say! He did land you a good one. What does Markham look like?"

George managed a lopsided grin but refused to say, and Adriana took advantage of his momentary silence to present him to Miss Courtland.

"I do hope you are not suffering too much," she said kindly, earning his instant admiration.

"No. It is merely a trifle," he said.

"It must hurt," put in Cecily, belatedly concerned.

"Only when I laugh," admitted George.

"It looks shockingly painful. And so ugly. How could you have been so careless as to let someone hit you in the face. If it were me I would have tried to get myself hit some place where it would not show," advised his heart's delight.

"Have you never heard of a lucky punch, Miss Hammond?" asked George in irritation.

"I daresay I have not. But then, I detest fisticuffs. And besides," she added in a most irritatingly superior manner, "I believe a gentleman shouldn't discuss such things with a lady."

"Well here," said Albert. "I am more than willing to listen. Tell me how Markham managed to land such a good one. Never thought he had it in him," he said, drawing George aside and pumping him enthusiastically for details.

Cecily was not used to being dismissed in so cavalier a manner, and she turned a look of wide-eyed amazement on Kate, who gave an eloquent shrug. "Really," muttered Cecily as dinner was announced, "men are the strangest creatures."

Dinner did credit to hostess and cook alike. The table itself was a feast for the eyes. The candlelight made the crystal goblets wink and sparkle. Linen napkins folded in the shape of mitres perched on fine Sevres china. And in the center was an elaborate centerpiece—a castle made of sugar.

But of course the stomach had to be considered, too. And surely no one's stomach could complain of neglect after indulging in a fine turtle soup, salmon and a turbot surrounded by smelts. This first course was followed by a saddle of mutton, then chicken, and tongue and ham, accompanied by boiled potatoes and green peas. Even the much hoped for ices made an appearance at the Wallingford dinner table.

George's split and swollen lip made it painful for him to eat, but that didn't bother him. He had been seated next to Cecily and was content to watch the play of candlelight on her pretty face.

Cecily would have preferred a large number around her cousin's table—consisting predominantly of her admirers. But as the meal progressed she found she was enjoying Adriana's small dinner party more than she had originally thought she would. She even found herself feeling cordial toward Adriana's bucolic cousin. Every time he smiled or tried to say something to entertain her she could tell it cost him great pain. "I am truly sorry you were hurt," she said finally. "Please do not think you need to talk to amuse me, for we are a very gay company tonight and I am content enough to listen to the others."

George, misinterpreting the spirit in which this was said, bristled. A gay and witty company, eh? Was he not gay and witty enough to talk to Miss Hammond? "As you wish," he replied, and clamped his lips together.

The offended look was not lost on Cecily. "Now, what can I have said to vex you?" she wondered aloud.

"Nothing at all. If you do not wish to speak to me, I am most happy to oblige." With that he turned his attention to his neighbor.

Cecily flushed at this unexpected reaction to her kind speech. A look of determination lighted her violet eyes and she turned to Albert, who was seated next to her, and begged him to tell her all about himself. Albert was happy to oblige and kept Cecily's feigned attention throughout the dessert and cheese.

The ladies left the gentlemen to their port and retired to the drawing room in a rustle of silks. Cecily glided out of the room as if she had not a care in the world, making sure to pause and brush an imaginary wrinkle from her gown, giving her admirers (one provoking one in particular) a last glance at her sweet, smiling profile. The smile left her as soon as she gained the drawing room, however. She sat on the sofa next to her friend and muttered, "Really, he is the rudest man alive."

"Why, how can you say so when he kept you so entertained throughout the entire last course," cried Kate.

"He certainly did not. He would not even speak to me. If that country bumpkin thinks he may snub me he has a thing or two to learn," she muttered.

"Country bumpkin!" declared Kate. "The man is a breath away from being a viscount."

"George?"

"George! But we were not speaking of Mr. Atherby." Understanding dawned. "Oh. I see we were. Why, Cecily, never tell me you are interested in him."

"I certainly shan't," declared Cecily. "I hope I know better than to throw myself away on a rude nobody with no fortune to recommend him. Mama is depending on me. Why, with the state of her health such as it is, it would most likely send her into a decline if I did not marry well." Cecily tapped her chin thoughtfully. "The honorable Mr. Eagan is a very nice man—in a loud sort of way. How many pounds has he a year, do you know?"

Kate stiffened. "No. I do not. I am sure it is not as much as Lord Spenser has."

"Most likely not," agreed Cecily. "And Lord Spenser is much more handsome."

"In a cold, classical style," agreed Kate. "I prefer a more open and friendly face."

Cecily studied her friend's nonchalant expression from under hooded eyes. "Such as, perhaps, Mr. Eagan's?"

"Or your cousin's," Kate countered and turned to the conversation.

Wallingford had his instructions, and the gentlemen didn't neglect their ladies for long. Once they had joined them Adriana begged her sister-in-law to entertain them at the pianoforte. Elizabeth graciously consented and performed the required song and an encore in her sweet soprano. But Elizabeth did not think highly of her voice and could not be persuaded to sing another. So the gentlemen appealed to Miss Courtland, who, knowing her limitations, politely declined all entreaties.

Cecily, however, knew no limitations and was easily persuaded by Albert to perform. Her family members were strangely quiet, something Albert could well understand once she began to sing. Her voice was thin and not altogether true, and midway through the first song her listeners were wearing frozen smiles and beginning to squirm in sympathy as she unsuccessfully tried for notes beyond her reach. George alone seemed to be genuinely enjoying the torture and begged for another song when Cecily had finished. Albert and Kate politely but less enthusiastically joined in and Cecily happily obliged. Before George could ask her to do another, Adriana quickly thanked Cecily and hustled her away from the pianoforte. "We shan't force you to strain your voice by asking you to sing yet another song."

"It is no strain, I assure you," said Cecily.

"Oh, it never feels so at the time, but if a lady is not careful she can do severe damage to her voice box and have a very sore throat next morning," replied Adriana sagely.

"Yes, that is true," Elizabeth concurred. "I have experienced just such a thing myself on more than one occasion. We should hate to see you do serious damage to your voice."

It never occurred to Cecily to question her advisors or to wonder how other singers such as the famous Catalini, whose voice currently rang out from the stage of the King's Theatre, could sing for long periods of time without damaging their voices. Taking her relative's advice, she sat down and patted her curls, well pleased with herself.

George was also well pleased with her performance, and was so lost in his contemplation of the lovely picture she had made that he didn't at first hear his name. "George," repeated his cousin. "Won't you please recite some Shakespeare for us?"

George had not planned on this. He blushed and shook his head.

"Oh, yes, Mr. Atherby," said Kate. "Your cousin and Lady Raine have been telling us you recite with great feeling."

George gave an embarrassed grin and shook his head.

"George," said Adriana with mock sternness. "Everyone who comes to our home must sing for his supper."

"Go on, old man," boomed Albert. "Pick something I know and I'll prompt you."

The other guests added their entreaties, but what made George get up was Cecily's taunting remark. "Really," she said, "if he feels incapable we should not force him."

"I am quite capable," he assured her.

Cecily gave him a superior look. "Then you should have no reluctance to show us."

George rose from his seat and strode purposefully to the center of the room. Suddenly he was no longer in a drawing room. He was in a garden—the Capulets' garden. *"But soft!"* he began, *"what light through yonder window breaks?"*

In spite of themselves the company followed George's glance and the motion of his hand. Cecily's mouth dropped. George's piercing stare caught her eyes and held them. ". . . *It is my lady; O, it is my love! O, that she knew she were!"*

Cecily began to blush under George's unfaltering gaze. Her hand went to her cheek but she was unable to tear her eyes away. She sat mesmerized as he continued.

". . . O, that I were a glove upon that hand, that I might touch that cheek!" When George stopped the room was filled with silence—then the sound of clapping and enthusiastic praise.

George continued to look at Cecily, who lowered her eyes demurely and blushed.

"A country bumpkin, is it?" whispered her friend. "Country bumpkin, indeed!"

• 5 •

George was a fair angler and he looked across the room, measuring Miss Cecily Hammond with a fisherman's eye. Surely the same principles must apply when one was attempting to win a woman, he reasoned. He had used the bait Adriana had offered to him, and Cecily had obviously risen to it. In spite of his bruised face, George knew she had been impressed with his oratory. If the eyes were truly the windows of the soul, then he was convinced he and Cecily had looked into each other's souls in those few minutes, and he was as sure she would be his as he was that the sun would rise the next morning. And he was sure Cecily knew it, too. But she would fight it. He would have to give her a lot of line, let her run a little before reeling her in. So he purposely ignored her for the rest of the evening, an action which caused her extreme irritation. As the evening wore on the lovely Cecily seemed to find smiling an effort. She became restless and began to tap her closed fan in her lap. George noticed this and smiled to himself. For the first time since meeting Miss Cecily Hammond he felt in control of a situation.

When the party came to an end he managed under cover of the hubbub all around them to kiss her hand and whisper, "Oh, that I were a glove!"

Miss Cecily Hammond, the young lady who was used to pulling the heartstrings of others and making them dance like puppets, squirmed uncomfortably. "If you were a glove I should shut you away in a drawer," she snapped, snatching her hand free.

George's smile was gently mocking. He bowed and her hand itched to add yet another bruise to that insolent face.

"Good night, Miss Hammond. I shall have pleasant dreams tonight."

"I hope you have nightmares," Cecily rudely replied and turned from him to bid her other guests farewell.

George left the party well pleased with himself. In his mellow mood it was easy for Albert to persuade him to "toddle on over to the club and see what's to do." George's new friends greeted him with an air of jovial acceptance, and he cheerfully frittered away the rest of the night and a good sum of money at the card table. By the time he finally found his bed he was too tired even to think of Cecily and his sleep was deep and dreamless.

Cecily wasn't so fortunate. The next day she confided to her friend Kate over a table piled with bolts of fabric in Grafton House that she had had the most unpleasant dream. "I dreamt I had become engaged to George and he had only bought me garnets for a betrothal present, and Mama had severe palpitations and told me I was an ungrateful daughter, and then Lord Spenser came along on a big white horse and laughed at me and told me if I had chosen him he would have bought me the largest diamond in all of England," She shuddered.

"I think your cousin is terribly sweet," said Kate. "Surely if you were to choose him your mama wouldn't mind so very much."

"*I* should mind!" declared Cecily. "He is clumsy and skinny and . . . and . . ."

"And he has a kind heart," chided Kate gently.

"So does Lord Spenser. And he has broad shoulders and a fortune besides. And a title."

"But does not your cousin inherit a title?"

"Pooh! A mere baronetcy."

Kate shrugged. "I suppose you are right. With your looks and fortune you could do better."

"I certainly can," agreed Cecily. "It is unfair to lead George on, though. I shall have as little as possible to do with him in the future."

Cecily soon began to realize this would not be an easy resolution to keep. It is because we are related, she told herself. One cannot completely avoid a relation, no matter how one tries, for they are always turning up. "Well, I shall be civil to him, but I shall not do anything to encourage him," she later confided in Kate.

Cecily never knew what possessed her to accept when George called one afternoon and proposed she and Adriana come riding with him the next day. But accept she did, and the next day she found herself sedately trotting down a tree-lined path in Hyde Park with Adriana and the man she had not intended to encourage. George caught her observing him from under her lashes and smiled tenderly at her. She blushed and tossed her curls, and, as if sensing her mistress' mood, the little mare she rode also tossed her head.

George loved to ride. He had been in the saddle almost as soon as he had walked, and he excelled at it. There was no more bruising rider to the hounds than George Atherby, and when he sat a horse he became a centaur.

Cecily couldn't help but admire how well he held the big animal with which Wallingford had mounted him. It pranced and snorted in a fierce manner that made Cecily nervous just to watch. "Does it not frighten you being on such a big, mean animal?" she finally asked.

"Mean? Old Firebrand here merely likes to show off,

that's all. But he and I understand each other." George patted the horse's neck and its ears went back as if to say, "Don't you believe him."

Adriana laughed. "I suspect you get along with him better than he does with you."

George smiled and the three rode on companionably, nodding to their various acquaintances. George was feeling mellow and content until a dashing figure on a large black horse rode into view.

"Oh, look. It's Lord Spenser!" cried Cecily, her eyes lighting up. George frowned as Lord Spenser cantered up alongside them.

George's horse obviously liked Lord Spenser's horse no better than his rider liked Lord Spenser, and took immediate exception to the big black, attempting to bite his flank. For a moment the two men were fully occupied in controlling their mounts. They finally positioned themselves with Cecily and Adriana between them. "That is quite a beast you have there, Atherby," said Lord Spenser, in a condescendingly cordial tone.

"He's Wallingford's," said George. "I like him quite well."

"He seems to be terribly mean," said Cecily. "I should hate to ride him."

"I am sure no one would want you to," said Lord Spenser.

"Big horses such as that one frighten me," Cecily confessed. "I prefer carriages."

"Do you like curricles?" asked Lord Spenser.

"Oh, yes!"

"Then perhaps Lady Wallingford will permit you to come driving in mine tomorrow," said Lord Spenser.

Adriana felt George's jealous glare burning over her shoulders, but politely replied that she had no objections.

"Do say you will drive out with me tomorrow, Miss Hammond," begged Lord Spenser.

Cecily's eyelashes fluttered downward and she peeped up at his Lordship from under their thick veil. "I shall be pleased to bear you company."

"Capital!" he said enthusiastically. "I shall look forward to the pleasure of your company. Shall I call for you at four o'clock?"

Cecily nodded.

Lord Spenser smiled at her then tossed a triumphant look at his competitor. "Till tomorrow then, Miss Hammond." He tipped his hat to Adriana. "It has been a pleasure Lady Wallingford, Atherby . . ." Lord Spenser touched his horse's flank and cantered off.

"Only look how well he sits a horse," declared Cecily as his Lordship rode away.

No one answered her. Adriana bit her lip and George seemed preoccupied with watching something on the other side of the park. Five minutes passed in silence, Cecily looking like the cat who swallowed the canary and George looking glum. Finally Adriana said, "I feel fatigued. Would you both mind if we turned back?"

"I have no objection," replied Cecily lightly.

"As you wish," murmured George listlessly.

They turned their horses and headed back in the direction they had come. After a few moments it was George's turn to perk up at the sight of a familiar face. "Here come Miss Courtland and Albert."

Kate and Albert and another young lady, whom Albert introduced as his cousin Amelia, rode up to them and stopped to exchange pleasantries.

"My, but you handle that horse in such a masterful way," Kate told George admiringly.

"He is a brute," put in Albert.

"Oh, he is probably no worse than Lord Spenser's horse," said George, still preoccupied with the unfortunate turn of the afternoon's events.

"Spenser's big black? Hah! The nag's all show. He's really rather a spiritless beast, don't you know? I think the only reason Spenser keeps the nag is to make himself look good."

"That is awful!" cried Cecily in reproving tones.

The reproof was lost on Albert. He shrugged nonchalantly. "Rather. But that's Spenser for you. Always likes to have the best—or at least look as if he does. I say, is everyone going to Lady Jersey's rout on Friday?"

"Is anyone *not* going would be a better question," laughed Kate. "Anyone who is anyone at all will most likely be there. I wonder how she will fit all her guests in her house."

"I don't know," said Cecily. "Just so I fit—that's all I care for. I would certainly hate to miss it."

"A rout is such a boring affair," Adriana said, sighing.

"Oh, but we are going, aren't we?" asked Cecily.

"Of course, goose. As you said, anyone who is someone will be there."

When Cecily went driving with Lord Spenser the next day she learned that he planned on attending, and after spending a very pleasant afternoon in that handsome young man's company, she very much looked forward to the coming Friday night.

George, on the other hand, was not sure if he was looking forward to the party or not. Much as he longed to see Cecily again, he didn't look forward to seeing her in a social setting. Even though no calamity had befallen him at his cousin's dinner party, his painful experience at Almack's was burned into his memory. He would have given anything to avoid Lady Jersey's rout, but he was sure Lord Spenser would be there and he knew if he was going to win Cecily he didn't dare abandon the field to his rival. But he definitely needed something which would give him an edge over the competition. What could he do that would enable him to steal a march on Lord Spenser? "There must be something I can do to impress her and show her I am not some green country yokel," he said to Albert the Thursday before the rout.

"I have it!" declared Albert. "Come with me," he commanded, and hustled George out his front door.

"Where are we going?" asked George, eager and curious.

"You'll see," Albert answered mysteriously. "I noticed right from the start that something was missing from your wardrobe," he said as they entered the establishment of Rundell and Bridge. "If you are going to be a proper town beau you must have a decent snuffbox."

"But I don't take snuff," objected George.

"Then learn, man! Hey ho, here's a nice one," Albert said, picking up a small enameled snuffbox and handing it to George.

"Yes, I like that," said George. "I'll take it," he told the clerk.

"And this one, too," said Albert, handing the man another.

"What the devil do I need with *two* snuffboxes?" George objected.

"Would you wear the same cravat every day?" asked Albert. George shook his head. "Well, then that is why you need more than one snuffbox. Petersham has one for every day of the week."

The two friends proceeded from Rundell and Bridge to Fribourg and Treyer, London's fashionable tobaccanists, where they spent the greater part of an hour deliberating over what kind of snuff to purchase for George. They finally settled on King's Martinique. "It's a trifle light in character," said Albert, "but you probably want that for now. Later on you can try something stronger. I mix my own."

George looked at his friend with admiration. "You do?"

Albert nodded. "If you want to experiment later I will be glad to help you."

Purchasing the snuff and snuffboxes had taken much of the afternoon. Learning the art of taking snuff was an equally absorbing task which took up the rest of the day and gave George a very red nose. "What is in this, pepper?" he complained after taking too much and sneezing several times.

Albert laughed. "You'll catch on, old fellow. Try again."

Soon George was taking the properly delicate pinch of snuff in such an elegant manner Albert assured him that all who saw him would think he had been doing so for years. He had even mastered that much-to-be-envied skill of opening his snuffbox using only his left hand. "That should impress Miss Hammond," said Albert.

"You think so?" asked George eagerly.

"Of course. If she ain't impressed then she don't know much," Albert replied sagely.

The day of Lady Jersey's rout arrived. Armed with a new skill and a great deal of hope, George readied himself for the event, taking great care in his toilet, and even going so far as to persuade Albert to come over and supervise the tying of his cravat. After much discussion, the gentlemen settled on the mathematical, an intricate style which Albert assured him would impress any fashion-conscious person, whether male or female. This took considerable effort and concentration, and fifteen discarded neckcloths lay on

George's dressing-room floor before the proper effect was achieved.

"There," said Albert, stepping back to admire his work. "Slap up to the nines."

George looked critically at himself in the glass. Most of his bruises had faded and his lips were again the proper size. His cravat was truly a work of art. His chest was still anything but massive, but there was little he could do about that. His valet helped him into his coat and he surveyed the final result of the efforts of three men to make him appear dashing.

"Yes, it will do quite well," said Albert approvingly.

"Do you really think so?"

Albert nodded. "Definitely. Let us go and take the citadel by storm."

George approached Lady Jersey's house at number 38 Berkeley Square with something approaching awe. London's elite would be here tonight. And to think he, George Atherby, would be one of them. Visions of conversations with great minds and introductions to some of England's most important political and social leaders danced in his head. Of course, the biggest treat of the evening would be seeing Cecily and basking in the warmth of her admiration when she saw how fine he looked.

And she did indeed admire his handsome attire. "How ever did you manage to tie your cravat so intricately?" she asked in awed tones.

"It wasn't easy," George said. "The mathematical is most difficult, you know."

"Oh my! Must you know mathematics to do that?"

George pondered this seriously. "A mathematical mind is a definite asset."

"Well, I must say, you do look very handsome tonight," Cecily said graciously. "And how do you like my new gown? Adriana does not think the color suits me, but I like it very well."

George took in the concoction of dark green with its abundance of ruffles and flounces. What little sleeve there was beautifully capped soft, plump arms and creamy shoulders. The neckline was scalloped and cut to allow a tantalizing glimpse of small breasts. Cecily's hair was held by tiny diamond clips that glittered in her dark curls like stars. "You look lovely," George said simply.

"I thank you, sir." Cecily curtsied. "I feel quite pretty in this, and I intend to have a very good time tonight. I only wish there was dancing. Oh, look, there is Sir Winston!"

George sighed inwardly. He had known all along the competition would be fierce, but he had been enjoying Cecily's undivided attention and had hoped to have her to himself for at least a few more minutes. He greeted his portly, middle-aged rival with great politeness, however.

Sir Winston eyed the skinny young man speculatively. He must have compared his merits with that of the younger man and felt himself the winner, for he smiled benignly on George after the introductions were made and asked him how he was enjoying his stay in London and what his plans for the future were.

George replied casually that he hadn't as yet made any definite plans. "I think I should like to stay in town till the end of the Season," he said, casually pulling out his snuffbox. With his best man-about-town air George held the snuffbox in the palm of his hand and flicked the lid open with his thumb. Unfortunately, he lost his grip on the box. It jumped out of his hand, sending a little cloud of tobacco floating to the floor. Cecily sneezed and moved her skirts.

George blushed and bent to retrieve it, trying in spite of his embarrassment to look nonchalant.

Sir Winston smiled condescendingly, and after George had replaced the runaway container and stood up, he pulled out his own snuffbox, and with an effortless flick, opened it, offering some to George. George took a pinch, sniffed and sneezed. "Thank you," he murmured.

"It is my own mix. I shall be happy to give you the recipe if you like it."

George smiled weakly, drew out his handkerchief and blew his nose. "Thank you," he said, wishing Sir Winston and his snuffbox to the devil.

Sir Winston once again turned his attention to Cecily. "Miss Hammond, I knew that color would become you. You look like Aphrodite just sprung from the sea in that lovely gown."

"Why, thank you, Sir Winston. What a pretty compliment."

"No more pretty than the lady to whom it was given, I assure you. And the diamonds in your lovely dark curls look like stars in the night sky."

"Oh, how lovely!" exclaimed Cecily, clapping her hands together.

"I thought that very thing myself," put in George.

"Then why did you not say so?" asked Cecily, obviously disbelieving.

George started to reply he did not say so because he had thought it would sound rather silly. But then he realized Sir Winston might take offense at such a remark. He was saved from having to answer Cecily by the arrival of Lord Spenser.

By now Cecily had seated herself on a gilt chair and she graciously held out her hand to the newest member of her court. "Lord Spenser, you are looking truly magnificent tonight." Lord Spenser smiled complacently at this compliment. "And your cravat is almost as impressive as George's," Cecily continued.

Lord Spenser surveyed George's cravat. "The mathematical, eh? Not an easy one to achieve. I congratulate you, Atherby." Having given Miss Hammond's country cousin all the notice he deserved, Lord Spenser returned his attention to Cecily. "May I say you are looking lovely tonight, Miss Hammond? In fact, you are the loveliest lady in the room."

"I am fast becoming the thirstiest," said Cecily. "It is so very warm in here!"

"Allow me to fetch you a cup of negus," offered George.

"I shall be happy to fetch it," said Lord Spenser. He sprang into action and headed across the room toward the butler, who was bearing a trayful of cups.

George glowered at his competitor and, not to be outdone, also darted across the room.

Sir Winston was no fool. He stood his ground and made good use of his rivals' absence by amusing Cecily with his vast store of gossip, witty sallies, and outlandish compliments.

Meanwhile, the two competitors had both procured a cup of punch and were racing back across the crowded room, each determined to be the first to reach Cecily with their prize. Lord Spenser had a head start on George, but George was able to narrow the gap when Lord Spenser was waylaid by a friend and stopped momentarily. It was soon obvious to everyone the two men passed that a race was on, and conversations began to soften and die as heads turned to watch the competitors speeding back across the room. Lord Spenser managed to dodge a portly gentleman, but was finally cut off by a turbaned dowager, who stepped away from her circle of friends and directly into his path.

He stopped short of knocking the lady over and smiled politely at her as he wiped sticky liquid off his fingers and waistcoat.

The finish was in sight. George smiled triumphantly back at his competitor, failed to see a gentleman's protruding leg, and promptly tripped over it. He struggled to keep his balance, plunging forward with three long-legged hops and setting a small table teetering dangerously in the process. Bouncing off the table, George caught his balance by grabbing Sir Winston's sleeve. Unfortunately, he did not succeed in keeping the negus safely inside the cup and it landed on Cecily. As the liquid trickled a dark path down her bodice, her countenance darkened to match. George hung his head.

"Oh," moaned Cecily. "It is so sticky and . . . ugh!"

"Here, my dear," said Sir Winston comfortingly, giving Cecily his handkerchief. "What a shame to have your pretty gown ruined."

Lord Spenser arrived on the scene and quickly offered her his stained coat. "Here, Miss Hammond," he said, wrapping it around her. "I shall find your cousin."

"Thank you," Cecily murmured sweetly, and Lord Spenser gave George a maddeningly superior smile before departing in search of Adriana.

Cecily's lips were pressed in a thin line. She mopped again at her damp gown. George began a stuttered apology, but she held up a hand to stop him. "Pray, do not bother to apologize," she said between clenched teeth. "In fact, I hope you may never talk to me again as long as I live. I certainly do not intend to speak to you." And with that she haughtily turned her head from him.

George slunk away to a far corner of the room from which he sadly watched a highly irritated Cecily being escorted from the party by Adriana and Wallingford. The sympathetic look Wallingford threw him as they shepherded their charge from the room was small comfort. George sighed and tried to smile apologetically at what seemed like a horde of staring, smirking faces. This is it, he thought glumly. I have ruined my chances for happiness.

"Rather bad luck," said a voice at his elbow.

George turned to see a very handsome man with large eyes and a finely chiseled nose standing next to him. The man was dressed in an elegantly simple coat and breeches. His waistcoat was pale blue and even to George's inexperienced eye the material looked expensive. A single diamond tiepin peeped out from the simple folds of a perfectly starched cravat.

"It is fortunate for the young lady that at least one of her friends had the courage to do something about that hideous gown," the man continued. "Of course, I wanted to admire her, but I found I could not, for that shade of green combined with those violet eyes was making me quite bilious. Perhaps her gown is ruined. We can but hope." With that the gentleman strolled off, leaving George gaping after him.

"Atherby," hissed Albert, coming up and grabbing George's arm. "When did you meet the beau?"

"The beau?" repeated George stupidly.

"George Brummell. Never tell me you were talking to the beau himself and didn't know it. Oh, that is famous!" Albert slapped his thigh. "What did he say to you? Did he like your cravat?"

"No," George answered slowly, still not fully comprehending the great honor just done him. "He said I did Cecily a great service by spilling punch on her—that the green did not go well with her eyes." George sighed. "I thought she looked beautiful."

"Oh, but that's rich," chortled Albert. "Here, Phinney, "

he said, grabbing a passing friend by the arm. "You will never guess what the beau just said to George." Before George could stop him, Albert had repeated the tale, and his friend's laughter drew more eager listeners into their circle to hear the story.

"I've lost her," George moaned later as he and Albert left Lady Jersey's house.

"Bah." Albert waved this observation aside. "Brummell has exonerated you. And once Miss Hammond hears the beau said that green clashes with her eyes she'll never wear the gown again. Depend on it."

"I don't care about the gown. I embarrassed her publicly. She will never forgive me for that."

Albert was silent.

"I'm going home," George announced.

"Good idea," said Albert. "A good night's sleep and things will look better in the morning."

"No," said George. "I mean *home*."

"What? Leave town in the middle of the Season? Don't be a fool, man. Why, you will miss Markham's card party next week."

"I don't care. I'm leaving. I am going back to the country where I belong."

"You belong here," said Albert.

George only shook his head sadly. What was the sense in staying in town? It would be like a beggar standing before a bakery. There was no sense in longing for what he couldn't have.

He went to his lodgings and drafted a note of thanks to his cousin for all her kindness to him during his stay in London, then proceeded, with the help of his valet, to pack as many bags as he could find. George looked at the mountains of clothes ranging around his room and realized he now possessed much more than he had originally brought with him, and was left with a dilemma. Finally he shrugged. "Well, I will have to buy a trunk or something tomorrow," he muttered. He gave up packing for the night, dismissed his man and went to bed, where he dreamed he was spilling cup after cup of negus on Cecily.

• 6 •

GEORGE FINALLY DRAGGED himself from sleep late the next morning. His heard hurt and he felt sick at heart. He kept hoping as his valet shaved him that his hand would slip. Unfortunately, the man had a hand as steady as a rock, and George soon found himself dressed with no choice but to face the new day.

He dispatched his message to his cousin and set off in search of a trunk. Shopping was a gloomy experience, and George came home feeling even worse than when he had left, a thing he would not have thought possible earlier that morning.

Seeing the envelope waiting for him on the silver salver did nothing to raise his spirits. He opened it and scanned its contents. As he suspected, it was from his cousin. "Do not leave until you have seen me," she ordered. "Cecily will be gone from home this afternoon. You may come at two o'clock."

The summons was impossible to ignore, mainly because it offered hope. George didn't really want to leave London. Perhaps Cecily wasn't as angry with him this morning as she had been the night before. Well, he would stay around just long enough to call on his cousin and bid her an official farewell. His trunk wouldn't be delivered till three, anyway.

At ten minutes before the hour George found himself being ushered into his cousin's drawing room. "Oh, you poor, dear boy!" exclaimed Adriana, leading him to the sofa. "You look as though you did not sleep a wink. I am so very sorry."

George shrugged. "It was merely one of those unfortunate accidents. Is Cecily still very angry?"

Adriana shook her head. "No. She has recovered. We have already heard about Mr. Brummell's comments, you see."

"News travels fast," George interrupted bitterly.

Adriana ignored this remark and continued, "She says it is probably just as well it happened since no one might otherwise have told her that her gown clashed with her eyes. But what sealed your pardon was the fact someone mentioned to her that the beau might not even have taken notice of her had you not attracted his attention with your accident."

George smiled knowingly at his cousin. "I wonder who it was."

Adriana returned his smile. "I suppose one can hardly blame her for being angry. It is never fun to be the center of attention in unpleasant circumstances. But Cecily was really very quick to forgive you."

George heaved a sigh of relief. "I never thought she would."

"Well, she has. Which is why I sent word for you not to leave town. I knew you were all upset and ready to give up."

George ran a hand through his hair. "Who wouldn't be? I made such a fool of myself I can never face her. In fact, I don't know how I can face anyone." George slammed his thigh in frustration. "It was such a curst stupid thing to do. And there was Spenser, just smiling at me in that superior way. Damn his teeth! Oh, beg pardon, coz," he said, flushing. He slumped back against the sofa cushions. "How could I have been so clumsy?" he moaned.

"There now," said Adriana, patting his hand. "It is over and done and you are allowing the incident to grow to much larger proportions than it deserves."

George only shook his head.

"There is still much Cecily does not know about you. And there is much you could do to win her admiration."

"Yes," agreed George bitterly. "I could fetch her another cup of punch next time we meet."

"No, but I have thought of something else you could give her."

George looked at his cousin skeptically. "What might that be?"

"A poem—perhaps an ode to her beauty? You know, you are quite good at that sort of thing, and what lady does not love to receive a poem from an admirer?"

George hesitated, not because he lacked confidence in his skill as a poet, but because he lacked confidence in his luck.

"Come now," prodded Adriana. "What could possibly go amiss in writing a poem for Cecily?"

"Nothing, I suppose. But after what has happened I would be too embarrassed to give it to her."

"I have it! Why not slip it to her at the Mayhew's ball on Friday?"

George gave a contemplative nod. "That might do."

"Oh yes!" cried Adriana. "How romantic to attend a ball and receive a love poem from an ardent admirer. Trust me, dearest. That is just the sort of thing to capture Cecily's heart. Now! Go home and get started right away," she said, taking his teacup from him and pulling him to his feet. "Let your imagination soar."

"I shall try," promised George.

"Good," replied his cousin, hurrying him out of the room and on his way.

Having solved the problem of George and his future, Adriana poured herself another cup of tea and settled back on the sofa with a satisfied smile.

"And what new plot have you and your dashing young cousin been hatching now?"

Adriana jumped. "Really, Gerald," she snapped, pouring the spilled tea on her saucer back into her cup. "I do wish you would stop sneaking up on me. It quite unnerves me."

The earl helped himself to a macaroon. "Is it not a little early for tea?" he asked.

Adriana ignored this remark and set her cup down. She poured her lord one and handed it to him.

"I met George on the steps," he said. "It would appear you have dissuaded him from leaving."

"I have."

"And when does the next attack take place?"

"Friday. At the Mayhew's ball."

"What will he spill on her there?"

Adriana was not amused. "Nothing. He is going to write her a poem."

"Our George has many talents."

"He does!" declared Adriana.

"I know he does," said Wallingford consolingly. "But I do wish, my love, that you would quit helping him exhibit them."

"You surely do not blame me for what happened at Lady Jersey's?"

"No. But I wish you would not take part in this farce."

"Are you putting your foot down?"

"No. Not yet. I should not like to reach a point where I must."

Adriana smiled at her husband. "You worry too much. You never used to."

Wallingford shrugged. "The role of chaperon is a dull one. I fear it is making me old and stodgy."

"You are not old and stodgy," Adriana assured him. "At least not so old and stodgy that you have forgotten what it is to be madly in love."

Wallingford gave his wife a sidelong glance and smiled in spite of himself. "A very clever tactical move," he said. "But come now. I said I would not put my foot down."

"That is what you said," agreed Adriana. "But nonetheless I can see it poised in midair."

"Frankly, love, I do not know how much longer I can bear to see your poor cousin suffer. And by helping him you only prolong the agony."

"Gerald, that is only your opinion. I am sure George would not agree with you."

Adriana was right. Rather than seeing his cousin's help as prolonging his agony, George saw her as an important ally and was grateful to her. He was sure the only reason Cecily did not wish his head on a platter was because Adriana had somehow miraculously intervened on his behalf and pleaded his case.

She hadn't—at least nothing more than sharing her observation on Mr. Brummell's words with Cecily. That had been enough to bring Cecily out of mourning for the ruined garment. After all, George Brummell, friend of the Prince Regent and arbiter of taste was someone to be listened to. His notice could raise a young lady's social status to dizzying heights. And his word on fashion must always be the final one. One casual remark of Beau Brummell's was worth a thousand of Sir Winston's compliments. The green gown had been given to Cecily's maid that very morning.

Unfortunately for George, while Cecily had forgiven him for ruining her gown and her evening, she had again adopted her earlier view of him. That very afternoon as she sat with her friend Kate, she declared she was sure she had imagined the forceful and romantic soul she had glimpsed the night of her cousin's party. "My first opinion of George Atherby was correct. He is nothing more than a country bumpkin," she said. The fact that Lord Spenser had been involved in the ill-fated race of the night before and had managed to spill punch on himself counted not at all against him. *He* had had the decency merely to spill it on himself.

But George, unaware of all this, went back to his lodgings with hope in his heart. Adriana's idea was a good one. George had a way with words and had often amused his family and friends with his doggerel. Obviously Cecily liked outrageous compliments. She had certainly lapped up all the drivel Sir Winston had given her at the rout. By Jove! George could talk about stars and goddesses as well as the next man. He ordered his valet to unpack his things and send back the trunk he had ordered. Then he sat down at his desk and began to write furiously. "Oh skies, have you lost your brightest star? You have looked both near and far. She is here, and shines in Albemarle Street. And all of London is at her feet." George picked up the parchment and read his handiwork. "Not a bad start," he said to himself. He set the paper down and chewed on his lower lip. Where to go from there? He almost wished he had listened more carefully to some of Sir Winston's compliments. What were some of the things he had said?

Two hours and twenty sheets of paper later George had a headache, but no poem. He got up and stretched and poured himself a glass of port. He downed that and poured another and returned to his labors, taking the decanter with him. The more he drank the more the words began to flow.

Finally his poem was done. He read it aloud, hiccuped and giggled. "This is so silly!" he declared to the window. "But it is good. Cecily will . . . hic . . . Cec . . . hic. It's good."

He set down his sheet of paper and poured himself yet another glass of wine, which he was about to toss down when Albert was ushered into the room.

Albert blinked in the semidarkness. "Why the devil aren't the candles lit?" he asked. "It is dark as a tomb in here. Cold, too."

"I didn't want to be disturbed," replied George. "Light the candles, Shivers," George ordered with a grand gesture. "Let us have some light and celebrate. I have just created a masterpiece."

"And a mess," said Albert, looking at the papers scattered on the floor around the desk.

George held up the nearly empty decanter. "Wine?" he asked politely.

"There's none left," Albert pointed out.

"That can be reme . . . hic . . . rem . . . hic . . . fixed. Shivers, my good man, bring some more port and let us lay the covers for two. Albert, you must dine with me and help me cel . . . cel . . . celebrate, for I have just written a poem as good as anything Lord Byron can boast."

"Why?" asked Albert, perplexed.

"It is for Miss . . . hic . . . Miss . . . Cecily. Let me read it to you." George shoved his friend into a nearby chair, gave him the remains of the wine decanter and read him his poem, highly punctuated by hiccups.

Albert was greatly impressed and said so. The fact that Albert was anything but a man of letters didn't bother George in the least. Albert knew greatness when he heard it. "When are you going to give it to her?" he asked.

"At the Mayhew's ball on Friday."

Albert nodded sagely. "Well, this should do the trick."

"Shall I write one for you?" George offered generously. "You could give it to Miss Courtland."

Albert's eyes lit up momentarily, then he shook his head. "No. Everyone knows I can't write that stuff."

George nodded in agreement. "You don't need it anyway," he said. "Miss Courtland likes you. I wish Miss Hammond liked me," he finished, his voice heavy with wine-induced self-pity.

"You wait," said Albert encouragingly. "This poem will win her heart."

The night of the ball a very nervous George couldn't bring himself to hand his offering to the beautiful Miss Hammond. She was surrounded by admirers for most of the evening, and George had no desire to be so conspicuous as to present his poem to her in front of a whole entourage of smirking competitors. So he bided his time, watching her glide amidst the colorful swirl of dancers, admiring her while she talked with the other debutantes, her dark curls glowing in the candlelight.

Finally the perfect moment presented itself. Cecily sat next to Adriana on a dainty gilt-edged chair, fanning herself. Most of the guests had returned from supper and were milling about visiting while the musicians tuned up. George politely picked his way through the throng to where the ladies sat. He bowed over Cecily's hand and surreptitiously dropped the folded parchment at her feet. "I know your every dance is bespoken so I won't presume to ask you to dance," he said. "But I did want to tell you how lovely you look tonight."

"Thank you," replied Cecily primly. Her mouth dropped as George retreated to the other side of the ballroom. "Why, how very odd! He did not even stay to visit."

"Perhaps he is afraid to," suggested Adriana. "Any time he is with you for longer than ten minutes something horrible happens."

Lord Spenser came up to the ladies. "I believe the next dance is mine," he said. "Miss Hammond, did you drop something?" He stooped and picked up the paper which lay at her feet.

"No, I did not," said Cecily, taking the piece of paper. "How very curious."

"Why don't you see what it says?" prompted Adriana.

Cecily unfolded the paper and read its contents. "Oh, how lovely! It is a poem." She read it again, her face a study in delight.

"Look, she likes it," Albert said, poking his friend in the arm. George smiled. He waited, expecting Cecily to look across the room and acknowledge his gift. Instead she smiled up at Lord Spenser.

"This is truly lovely. I have never been compared to a shooting star before," Cecily told Lord Spenser as she tucked the poem safely away in her beaded reticule.

Lord Spenser looked a trifle confused, but rallied quickly. "Then it is high time you were," he said gallantly, offering her his arm.

Cecily smiled admiringly at Lord Spenser and allowed him to lead her onto the floor. "I shall treasure this poem always," she told him.

Lord Spenser merely smiled at her. Obviously, some mistake had been made, but as he was profiting by it, he saw no reason to disabuse Miss Hammond of her misconceptions. He reminded himself that all was fair in love as well as war. Besides, Miss Hammond would most likely not believe him if he denied having written the thing, anyway.

George watched this exchange, a look of increasing alarm growing on his face. "She thinks he wrote it."

"Nonsense," said Albert. "How could she?"

"Because I never signed it."

"You what?"

George shrugged helplessly. "I never dreamed Spenser would come along on my heels and grab the glory."

Albert's lip curled in disgust. "It looks as though this round is going to go to Spenser."

• 7 •

ADRIANA DIDN'T LEARN that her plan had backfired until she, Cecily, and Wallingford were in their carriage and on their way home. Cecily was still wound up and chattering about her evening's adventures. Adriana smiled politely and nodded her head, but she was tired and her mind kept drifting in and out of the conversation. She had fallen into a state of sleepy semiconsciousness when something Cecily said dragged her back. "What did you say?" she asked.

"I said the poem Lord Spenser wrote me was beautiful."

"Lord Spenser? How did you know it was Lord Spenser who wrote it? Did he sign it?"

"No. But, don't you remember? He was standing right there when I found it. In fact, he pretended it was something I had dropped. Wasn't that clever of him?"

"Yes," said Adriana, looking at her husband, who gave her a fatalistic shrug. Her eyes narrowed. "Very clever indeed," she muttered.

Adriana's maid had just unpinned the last curl from her hair when the expected knock came from the door leading to her husband's dressing room. She dismissed her maid and bid him enter. "If you have come to say I told you so you may march right back to your own bed this minute," she told him.

Wallingford shoved his hands into his dressing-gown pockets and grinned at her. "It does rather prove a point, does it not? You realize your helpful scheme has allowed George's rival an advantage he would never have had."

"Gerald!"

"I am sorry. I could not resist. I really came to console you," Wallingford said, flopping down on her bed.

Adriana came and sat next to him. "Lord Spenser has not won her yet, you know."

"Would it be so very awful if he did? After all, he seems nice enough . . ."

"But it would break George's heart if Cecily married Lord Spenser."

"Perhaps it would break Lord Spenser's heart if Cecily married George," suggested Wallingford.

Adriana shook her head. "No. Lord Spenser is a young man who appears to be very much accustomed to having whatever he fancies. At the moment he fancies Cecily, but I doubt his heart is seriously engaged. I *know* George's is."

Wallingford shook his head. "Poor George," he said, sighing.

The subject of this conversation was also doing his share of sighing over the discouraging state of his romantic affairs. Seeing Lord Spenser reap the benefits of his hard labor that night had been more than he could bear and he had taken leave of his hostess shortly afterward. But not before making his highly indignant friend promise he would say nothing about the poem's true authorship to Cecily. "But it ain't right!" objected Albert.

"I know. But a pretty fool I would look to Cecily if I made a big to-do over it," said George. "Promise me now—on your honor."

"Oh, dammitall, all right. If that's what you truly wish."

"It is," replied George.

"It goes against the grain to let Spenser get away with such a dirty trick," said Albert.

George sighed and shrugged. He looked mournfully at his beloved waltzing with Lord Spenser, smiling up into his face. It should have been him looking into those lovely violet eyes. "I am going home," he told Albert.

"I say, I'll come with you. This is the flattest affair I've been to all season," said Albert.

George laid a restraining hand on his friend's arm. "There is no reason you should leave this flat affair. Isn't Miss Courtland promised to you for the next dance?"

Albert feigned nonchalance. "Yes, but . . ."

"No." George shook his head. "I will be fine alone, I promise."

Albert looked at his friend seriously. "Are you sure?"

"Yes. I only *feel* like throwing myself from London Bridge. I am not really going to do it."

Albert clapped his friend on the back and sadly watched him leave the room.

George trudged back to his lodgings in Jermyn Street carrying a heavy heart. He had poured himself into writing that poem! Much good it had done him. Cecily took the poem but rejected him. He had sowed and Lord Spenser had reaped. He was no closer to winning Cecily than he had been when he first met her. And to make matters worse he had just unwittingly aided his rival. Why hadn't he signed that poem? Fool!

George dismissed his valet and undressed himself. He tried to avoid seeing the skinny frame reflected in his looking glass as he stripped off his shirt, but he was drawn to it like a magnet. He glared at himself. Lord Spenser most likely didn't glare when he saw his reflection. George hurled his shirt on the floor and kicked it across the room.

The next morning he awoke determined to retrieve the trunk he had sent back. Another summons from his cousin stopped him and he once again went to see her with a mixture of dread and hope.

"I know you are feeling downhearted," she said, drawing him to the sofa. "But you mustn't give up. You really mustn't. We will think of something. Promise me you won't be discouraged and run away."

George stiffened. "I would not be running away if I left. I only came to town for a visit. If I choose to end my visit early there is surely nothing cowardly in that."

"George, promise me you will remain for the Season," said Adriana. George sat rigid. "You must promise," she said sternly.

Cecily entered the room at this moment. "Oh, I didn't know you had company." She looked from George to Adriana. "Am I interrupting something? What must George promise?"

George squirmed and his cousin answered for him. "George was thinking of ending his visit and going home."

"Leave in the middle of the Season? Why ever would you want to do that?"

"Seeing you this morning I am asking myself the very same thing," said George, inspired. Then he had an idea. "And may I say again how lovely you looked last night? When I saw you I thought the sky had lost its brightest star."

"Why, that is the first sentence of the poem Lord Spenser wrote for me," declared Cecily. "Did he show it to you?"

"No," snapped George, all tenderness draining from his voice. "And how do you know Spenser wrote it?"

"I know he wrote it because he gave it to me. And if he did not show it to you how did you know that line? I must say it is very shabby to try and take credit for something another man has done."

George bristled. "It certainly is. Home is looking better

all the time." He jumped to his feet as though he'd been stuck with a pin. "I will bid you ladies good day."

"Really, your cousin is the strangest man," Cecily told Adriana after George had left.

"Perhaps you hurt his feelings," suggested Adriana.

"Hurt his feelings? Oh, I daresay you mean about the poem. Well, if I did it was no more than he deserved," said Cecily. "What a low thing to do—trying to steal the words from something Lord Spenser wrote."

"Suppose," said Adriana slowly, "Lord Spenser did not write that poem."

"Then who? Oh, heavens! You think your cousin wrote it? But if he wrote it why was it Lord Spenser who gave it to me?"

"I cannot answer that. I can only ask if Lord Spenser did not show George the poem how did George know the first line from it?"

"Oh, I don't know!" declared Cecily crossly. "But I shall ask Lord Spenser about it next time I see him."

"That is a good idea," Adriana said, and changed the subject.

"It was all I could do to keep from telling her," she said to her sister-in-law later that day as they circled Hyde Park in Lady Elizabeth's smart Park Phaeton. "But I could hardly admit to knowledge of George's authorship of the poem for fear my part in the whole thing would come out." She shook her head. "Pity. It was quite good, actually. Cecily showed it to me." Adriana twirled her parasol thoughtfully. "Lord Spenser obviously had no idea what Cecily was talking about when she began jabbering at him about the poem. How unfortunate for George that Lord Spenser had the presence of mind to pretend he knew what she was talking about. If only he had asked her what she meant."

Elizabeth reined in her horses to greet an acquaintance. That done she gave the reins a gentle slap and the ladies moved forward again and resumed their conversation. "Well, what's to do?" asked Elizabeth. "This courtship is looking more and more like it can only end in failure."

"Yes," agreed Adriana. "I think we have reached a point where desperate measures are required."

" 'Tis a pity we cannot provide George with an opportunity to cast himself in a heroic role. If he could save Cecily from something—drowning, a runaway carriage, highwaymen . . ."

"That is it!"

"What?"

"Highwaymen!" exclaimed Adriana.

Her sister-in-law looked at her as though she had taken leave of her senses. "I am not personally acquainted with any highwaymen, otherwise I would beg one to meet us on Hounslow Heath so your cousin could hit him over the head."

Adriana dismissed this remark with an airy wave of the hand. "We have no need of a real highwayman. I know of two large men who would look very fearsome with scarves across their faces."

Elizabeth stared at her sister-in-law for a moment, then understanding dawned and she caught the twinkle in Adriana's eyes. "Oh, yes." She chuckled. "I do believe that would serve."

"I shall talk to Gerald this evening. Cecily goes to the opera with Miss Courtland and her mama and papa tonight, and Gerald and I will have a quiet evening at home."

"Charles and I dine at Milford House tonight," said Elizabeth. "After an evening of good companionship and equally good port he will be in a most amenable mood."

Adriana giggled. "It will be such a wonderful adventure.

I only hope our husbands have not become so stodgy that they fail to recognize its merits."

Lord Wallingford had obviously become very stodgy; when Adriana first mentioned her plan (at a very opportune moment), he thought it a joke. He left off kissing her shoulder, lay back on her bed and laughed. "That is rich, my love, truly rich. But pray, how did we get on the subject of your cousin and mine at a time like this?"

Adriana turned to face him. "We were saying we wished everyone could be as happy as we."

Wallingford cocked an eyebrow at his wife. "*You* were saying that. I was otherwise occupied."

Adriana snuggled against his chest and looked at him with soft, pleading eyes. "Gerald," she murmured. "It is such a small thing to ask for George's happiness—for my happiness."

Wallingford stroked her arm. "No, my dearest. It is not a small thing. We would frighten Cecily to death. And if we didn't, who's to tell? Someone who really meant you harm might accost you. You would have to do away with your customary outriders and that would leave you very vulnerable, not to mention making you look incredibly eccentric."

"I should not care if I looked eccentric," said Adriana. "After all, Gerald, how many members of the ton can you name who are not?"

"What if a real highwayman were to waylay you before we could get to you?"

"We would plan it carefully so nothing happened."

"It is too risky."

"Gerald . . ."

"No. I am now putting my foot down, Adriana. No. And that is final."

Adriana suddenly lost all interest in laying in her husband's arms. She sat up and turned her back on him.

A frown temporarily darkened Lord Wallingford's handsome features. "How your ardor has cooled, my dear."

"I find it hard to delight in your company, my lord, when I know my happiness is of no real interest to you."

"I see. In that case, my dear, I will bid you good night." Lord Wallingford left her bed and her room. In spite of his irritation he couldn't help chuckling when he heard the solid thud of a hairbrush against the door he had just closed.

A few streets away in Berkeley Square, Lady Elizabeth was faring no better than Adriana. "I may be in my cups," said her lord, "but I am not so foxed that I would agree to such a crackbrained scheme as this."

"Charles, how can you be so unfeeling?"

"Come, Bess," said Lord Raine, slipping his arms around his wife's waist and burrowing his lips in her hair. "Let us not talk of this anymore."

"Very well," said Elizabeth lightly. "I am sure Gerald will be able to manage well enough without your help."

"Never tell me Gerald has agreed to this!" exclaimed Raine.

"I will tell you no such thing, for you asked me not to talk of it anymore," his lady replied, standing on tiptoe to plant a kiss on his chin. Then she danced from his arms and shed her wrapper, wearing the smile of a woman who knows her efforts have not been in vain.

The next day Raine tracked his brother-in-law down at Jackson's. Wallingford had just had a go with the gentleman himself and was toweling off his damp upper torso. He grinned at Charles and clapped him on the back. "Are you feeling the need of some exercise, Charles?"

"No. I am, however, feeling the need of some conversation with you."

Wallingford shrugged into his shirt and grinned. "I think I can guess the nature of this conversation."

"I am sure you can. What is the verdict, Gerald? Do we turn highwaymen for a night?"

"Certainly not. A more ridiculous idea I have never heard. I have done some idiotic things, but even in my wildest days . . ." Wallingford shook his head and began to laugh. "They really are imaginative, those wives of ours. I suppose my sister had you convinced I was committed to this scheme."

"Well, yes, as a matter of fact, she did."

"I declined the offer last night. And I can tell you it cost me dearly."

Charles chuckled. "I'll wager it did. Ah, well, it would have been fun. Are we turning into old men already?"

"I am afraid so," replied Wallingford. "At least, if my wife is to be believed we are."

Elizabeth was sorely disappointed to learn at teatime that her husband and brother were both declining to participate in the great adventure their wives had planned for them. "I had thought Adriana more capable of handling Gerald," she muttered.

"What was that?" asked her husband.

Elizabeth favored him with a look of displeasure. "It is really too bad of you," she scolded. "What are we to do now?"

"Two such resourceful ladies as yourselves? I am sure you will think of something," replied Raine.

"It is really too bad of them to be so uncooperative," she said as she and Adriana conferred at a rout later that evening.

Adriana watched her cousin flirting with Lord Spenser on the far side of the room. Obviously Cecily had forgotten to ask him about his authorship of her love poem. Adriana frowned. Elizabeth followed her gaze and sighed in sympathy. When her eyes returned to her sister-in-law's face it was to see a slow smile spreading across it. "I am not sure," said Adriana, "that we must yet give up our plans. I believe Cecily may still meet up with a highwayman."

Elizabeth looked at her in surprise. "Who?"

Adriana leaned over and whispered gruffly behind her fan, "Stand and deliver!"

• 8 •

ELIZABETH'S EYES GREW wide. "You do not mean what I think you mean, surely," she whispered.

"It will be the simplest of things, really," Adriana assured her. "I had a letter only last week from Aunt Mary, begging us to come visit her at Merrywood and bring George. She hasn't seen him since he was a baby. And you will never guess where she lives."

Elizabeth's eyes twinkled. "I can guess this much," she said. "You must cross Hounslow Heath to reach her estate."

Adriana smiled. "You are most perceptive. Hounslow Heath has always been a favorite haunt for highwaymen, so it would hardly be surprising if we were to encounter one. Now," she said, suddenly businesslike, "we have much to plan. Should Charles care if I were to slip over tomorrow morning for a cozy chat? I am in need of some new gowns and must have your advice."

"I should be delighted," replied Elizabeth.

"Delighted to do what?" asked a deep voice at her elbow.

In spite of herself Elizabeth gave a guilty start on turning around to find her husband by her side. "Charles! What are you doing here?"

"I came with you," replied Raine. "Have you forgotten?"

Elizabeth made a face. "Go away, do."

Charles eyed the two women suspiciously. "What new scheme are you two hatching?"

"None whatsoever, I assure you," said Elizabeth innocently. "But we can hardly gossip about our husbands when one of them is standing next to us. Do be a love and fetch me some punch."

Raine smiled and shook his head and took himself off. "I'll swear they are up to something," he told Lord Wallingford.

"At least the highwayman scheme has been abandoned," said Wallingford. "Whatever new plot they are hatching cannot be any worse than that."

The next morning the two women met to plan George's daring rescue of Cecily. Adriana had brought her fashion plates, which would provide a good cover should Charles happen to surprise them at work, and drawings of the most tempting walking gowns, tea gowns, and evening dresses lay scattered unheeded on the sofa and floor.

"I shall develop an awful megrim right before we are to leave and you will all proceed without me. You must make sure you leave Aunt Mary's at precisely ten o'clock so we do not miss each other."

"You will be all alone. What if you should meet a highwayman?" asked Elizabeth.

Adriana shook her head. "We are going to do this as close to Merrywood as possible, so I am sure I will be safe enough. I will accost you almost as soon as you are on the heath. I suppose I shall have to bribe one of the stable boys to accompany me. It might be a little terrifying to ride all the way to London alone."

"I should say so," agreed Elizabeth, her eyes wide. "Perhaps we had best not do this after all."

"I shall be safe enough, never fear," Adriana assured her.

Elizabeth relapsed into thoughtful silence. "There is only

one other problem," she said at last. "Charles and Gerald will be with us and they are liable to shoot you."

"You will have to find a way to warn them right before you all leave Merrywood that I will be making an appearance. And instruct them to pretend to be willing to give me what I want so George can appear brave."

"Are you sure George will agree to this scheme?"

"No," said Adriana frankly. "Which is why we must not tell him until the last minute. He will not wish me to appear foolish. That coupled with an opportunity to shine in Cecily's eyes should guarantee his cooperation."

Elizabeth clapped her hands in delight. "Oh, but this will be fun!" Then, glancing at the illustrations next to her she said, "Where will you get the clothes? You surely cannot wear any of Gerald's. You would be lost in them. And besides, they are much too fine."

"Yes, I have thought of that. I shall borrow some from John."

"Who will go straight to Gerald," Elizabeth objected. "You know how head grooms are. Their loyalties are always with our husbands."

"I have thought of that," said Adriana. "I will tell him my cousin needs them for a part in a home theatrical. A head groom would not hesitate to betray his mistress to his master if a horse were involved. But when it comes to clothes and theatricals? Believe me, the subject will never come up."

"Excellent," declared Elizabeth. "I do begin to believe this plan might work. If only we may find a way to keep you safe."

"Never worry. I shall make sure every precaution is taken to ensure my safety. I want to live to enjoy the success of all my careful planning and attend George and Cecily's wedding. Cecily is a great fan of Mrs. Radcliffe, and an adventure such as this must surely win her for George."

"Let us hope Gerald does not throttle you. I should hate to see you miss your moment of triumph," said Elizabeth.

Adriana laughed. "Oh, Gerald will be highly displeased, most likely. But not for long. When he sees how well my scheme has worked, he will have to admit he was wrong to be such a fussy old worrybag."

"I am sure you are right," agreed Elizabeth. "I only hope we may not scare Cecily too much."

Cecily was at that moment curled up in bed with hot chocolate and a novel about a young lady who seemed to have the most amazing adventures, including being locked up in a moldering old castle by a wicked uncle. Rescued by a strong, handsome hero, her escape had truly been inspired, and Cecily turned the last page of the book with regret.

Snuggling down under the covers she wondered wistfully why it was only pretend people who had such exciting things happen to them. She began to mentally catalogue her experiences since she had come to London. The number of dinners, balls, routs, ballet and opera performances she had attended was almost staggering. And they had been great fun. After all, what girl could find it boring to wear pretty gowns and have so many gentlemen vying for her attention and paying her pretty compliments. Yes, it was all great fun, but it all became rather ordinary after a while.

She searched her mind for any out of the ordinary experiences she had had and suddenly a youthful face with the most piercing eyes came unbidden to mind. He was reciting Shakespeare and looking at her in a most intense and compelling manner. Oh, no! I will not think of George Atherby, she told herself. He is certainly not dashing enough to qualify as an adventure.

Again she taxed her memory for any exceptional experience she had had since coming to London. Again, George Atherby came to mind. She could still picture it all so clearly. The look of panic on his face, the feel of the sticky punch as it seeped through her bodice. She frowned. Good heavens! Were the only unusual experiences she'd had connected with *him*? She drummed the coverlet with her fingers. He really was the most irritating man. It seemed every time she saw him he brought out the worst in her. And what was he, anyway? A mere nobody with no title or fortune to speak of. What would her mama say if she were to make such an inglorious match? All those years of planning wasted. Of course, this was a silly way to be thinking. She had no interest in George Atherby.

Her thoughts turned to Lord Spenser. Now, if ever there was a man meant to be the hero of a novel, surely it was him. Such a handsome face. Such fine, broad shoulders. Just the kind of man who would stop at nothing to rescue a lady from perilous circumstances. And so romantic. How could she have forgotten the beautiful poem he wrote for her. Why, that should have been the first thing to come to mind when tallying her London experiences, not the image of some silly, skinny man talking about moons and gloves. She sighed. How nice it would be to have an adventure.

How fortunate for the unsuspecting Cecily that her cousin's wife had taken an interest in her affairs! That morning Adriana came home and wrote two letters. One was directed to her Aunt Mary, thanking her for her kind invitation to dinner and naming the Saturday night two weeks following as most convenient for her family. Would this be acceptable to Aunt Mary? And would she mind terribly if her niece imposed and brought along her husband's cousin who was staying with them for the season, and Lord Wallingford's sister and her husband? Adriana smiled at this. Her aunt was a garrulous old woman who always delighted in seating as many as possible at her table. What a godsend Aunt Mary was!

Next Adriana penned a quick note to George demanding his presence at the upcoming event and carefully omitting any mention of the great adventure in store for him. Her next order of business was to dispatch a message to John, telling him she wished to see him on the morrow. Adriana smiled, pleased with herself. Really, it was a most clever plan.

Wallingford was also feeling very pleased with himself. He had heard no further mention of his wife's crazy scheme and was pleased that she had abandoned it so easily. She was no longer angry with him—a pleasant relief in itself. "It is not like her to give up so easily on something she has her heart set on," he admitted to his brother-in-law at White's the following week. "But I must say it is a relief."

"Do you know Bess has not mentioned another word about it either," said Raine. "That is not like her."

The two men looked at each other. "What could they be up to?" asked Wallingford.

"I don't know, but I'll wager this matter is not as dead as we would like to think it," said Raine.

Wallingford knew the matter was not dead when his head groom mentioned in passing a few days later that he hoped the clothes he gave her ladyship fit her cousin.

"Clothes? John, why was my wife borrowing clothes for her cousin?"

"She said something about him needing 'em for some play, your Lordship."

"A theatrical. Did Lady Wallingford mention when this was to take place?"

John scratched his head. "Don't think so. Only said she'd get 'em back to me in a week or two."

"Thank you, John," said Wallingford. He entered his library and, sitting behind his desk, propped his chin on his hands and began to make a mental catalogue of his social engagements for the next two weeks: a trip to the opera, Almack's, dinner at Aunt Mary's . . . Aunt Mary! Aunt Mary, who lived in splendor far from the noise of town, across . . . Hounslow Heath! Wallingford slammed his hand on the desk. The vixen! What was she up to? He rang for Hastings.

"Yes, my lord?"

"Is my wife at home?"

"I believe so, my lord."

"Please ask her to join me."

"Very good, my lord."

Wallingford planted himself on his desk, his back to the door, and tried to temper his warring emotions. Part of him was extremely angry. The other part couldn't help but admire his wife's spirit. The minx!

The library door opened and Adriana entered. Wallingford came round the desk and took her hand, planting a kiss on her palm. "You look lovely today, my dear."

"Thank you, my lord." Adriana gave him a curtsy.

"Of course, you look lovely in all your gowns," he continued, leading her to a chair. "And I imagine you will look equally fetching in John's clothes."

Wallingford smiled as a variety of expressions chased across his wife's beautiful face. First came shock, then dismay and, finally, too late, feigned innocence. "Whatever can you mean, Gerald?" she said, dropping into the chair.

"Come now, my love. You know exactly what I mean. There is no sense playing for time, for I have found you out." He seated himself on the edge of his desk and watched her, carelessly swinging one elegantly booted leg.

Adriana raised her chin. "I really have no idea what you mean," she said.

"You know very well what I mean. What were you planning to do, acquire a headache right before we were to leave for Merrywood?"

In spite of herself Adriana's mouth dropped.

"Really, my love, I am not so stupid as you might think."

Adriana hung her head. "Oh, Gerald. Are you terribly vexed?"

Wallingford chuckled in spite of himself. "I should be more vexed with you than I am. Really, my dear, do you intend to do this sort of thing every time I deny you something?"

"Oh, no, Gerald! How could you even think that of me? But this was so important. George's—"

"—Happiness is at stake," finished Wallingford. "And would you take such a risk if my happiness was at stake?"

"You should not have even to ask me such a thing," Adriana replied.

"You know I cannot allow you to do this," said Wallingford. Adriana started to speak, but he held up his hand. "Not," he continued, "when I myself have a strong desire to play the highwayman."

"Oh, Gerald!" Adriana jumped up and threw herself into her husband's arms. "Do you really mean it?"

"Yes. I am still worried about the safety of all involved in this little adventure. So we will take certain precautions. Samson will take John with him on the box and they will each have loaded guns. And *I* shall choose the spot where the robbery will take place."

"You must at least allow us to reach Hounslow Heath!" declared Adriana. "It will hardly be an adventure if we are set upon before we have barely passed through Auntie's gates."

"I will allow you to gain sight of Hounslow Heath," promised his Lordship, and his wife had to content herself with that.

"Gerald," she asked meekly, "would you have been so very angry with me if my plan had succeeded?"

"What do you think?"

"I think," sighed Adriana, "it is fortunate for me I was discovered."

"I think so, too," agreed her husband. "Ah, well, I do believe Charles had a secret desire to be a highwayman all along."

• 9 •

GEORGE HAD READ the latest note from his cousin with the usual mixed feelings. The lure of an evening spent in Cecily's company was one he knew he would be unable to resist. Yet why, he wondered, was he so bent on punishing himself? For punishment it would be. Surely the way his luck was running, if he spent an evening in Cecily's company some new mishap was bound to occur. Misfortune dogged his heels every time he came near Cecily. But George was by nature an optimist. "I may as well go," he told Albert, as they made their way to Fives Court to watch a boxing exhibition. "It is, after all, only a simple dinner at our great-aunt's. What could possibly go wrong?"

Albert shrugged. "Can't think of a thing, except highwaymen. But that is much better than being set on by footpads. Bloody nasty, footpads."

George thought that highwaymen sounded rather nasty, too, but he had kept that thought to himself, fearing Albert would mistake practicality for cowardice.

Cecily's feelings regarding the outing were not mixed at all. She simply wasn't looking forward to it. "But what will we do?" she asked Adriana.

"We will have a splendid dinner and we shall visit."

"Is your great-aunt very witty and amusing?" asked Cecily hopefully.

"Actually no," admitted Adriana. "But I think you will like her nonetheless."

Cecily looked rather dubious but said nothing.

"I know it sounds like a tedious way to spend an evening, but you may be pleasantly surprised before the night is over," said Adriana encouragingly.

Cecily sighed. "I hope so." She set down her embroidery and looked out the drawing-room window at the spring drizzle. "Life has seemed rather flat lately."

"We haven't seen much of George," mused Adriana.

"I would as lief do without the kind of excitement he brings," snapped Cecily.

Adriana's face showed disapproval.

"Oh, I am sorry," Cecily said, instantly penitent. "I should not say such things about your cousin, should I?"

"Not when he has such high regard for you and has done nothing but try to please you," said Adriana gently.

"Yes, I suppose you are right," said Cecily. "But really, it is hardly the kind of excitement a girl dreams of—having her gown torn and punch spilled on her."

Adriana had to agree. "Perhaps he will manage to avoid any catastrophies this time. I am sure we will have a most memorable evening."

Unbeknownst to Cecily, her family had worked out the details of a plan guaranteed to make her evening memorable. The night of the party was a clear and warm one, and the promise of a full moon would make the return trip very enjoyable. Cecily had cheered herself with the thought that her cousin Gerald and his charming brother-in-law would both be members of the party, and was cherishing hopes of coaxing them into a game of charades after dinner. Her face fell when Adriana told her that Wallingford had been called away overnight on estate business. "And I was hoping he would play at charades with us," she said wistfully.

"Well, never mind," said Adriana, patting her hand. "We shall still have Charles and George."

"Yes, that is true," said Cecily, brightening. But again Cecily's face fell when Lady Elizabeth arrived alone. "But where is your husband?" she asked.

Elizabeth shook her head. "He is in bed with a putrid sore throat. I am sorry I did not let you know," she said to Adriana. "It came on him so suddenly—late this afternoon. The doctor has seen him and he is resting now. Of course, I had planned to stay home and sit with him, but he insisted I come. He did not want to have my evening spoiled."

"Mine is," sighed Cecily. "Both Cousin Gerald and Charles absent. What a flat evening this will be." Her companions smiled at each other, but Cecily did not see.

Just then George was admitted to the room. He looked very fine in his evening breeches and dark coat, and looking at him Cecily gave a mental shrug. He was better than nothing. In fact, she thought, eyeing him from under her lashes, he really did look quite dashing. His hair had been cut in a new style—the Brutus—and was close cropped to his head, emphasizing the strong line of his chin and making him look older. He bowed and smiled shyly at Cecily and, feeling sorry for the things she had said about him earlier in the week, she favored him with a smile and complimented him on his dashing new hair style.

"Do you like it?" asked George eagerly. "It is all the crack, you know," he added.

"Yes, I know," said Cecily, not wanting to be thought ignorant of any matter of fashion. "It becomes you."

George thanked her, then looking around asked where the other two members of their party were.

"They were not able to come," said Adriana. "Gerald was called away on estate business and Charles is at home sick in bed, so to you alone falls the duty of escorting us. I hope you may not find it too taxing."

"I shall find it great fun," said George with a wide smile. "Three lovely ladies all to myself. How fortunate can a man be?"

Elizabeth patted their escort's arm. "Very prettily said, sir. A dashing new hair cut and such pretty compliments. You are turning into quite the town beau. I fear before the Season is over you will have to fight the ladies off with a stick."

George blushed at this and his harem giggled.

"I suppose we had best be on our way," said Adriana. "Oh, Cecily. I have forgotten my gloves. Would you mind terribly fetching them for me? They are on my dressing table."

Cecily obliged and left the room. Adriana went to the door, peeked out to make sure her charge was safely on her way up the stairs, then shut the door. She ran back to George, who was looking perplexed, and took him by the arm. "Now, George, we haven't much time, so listen carefully. Gerald is not out of town. He is at this moment having dinner with Charles at the club."

George's mouth dropped. "But— "

"Ssh," commanded Adriana. "As I said, we have not much time. The reason they are not here is because later tonight on our way home from Aunt Mary's they are going to waylay us."

George's eyes popped out. "What!" he exclaimed.

"Ssh!" hissed both ladies at once.

"They are going to pretend to be highwaymen and rob us as soon as we have reached Hounslow Heath," Adriana continued. "You will stand up to them. Gerald always carries pistols in the carriage. Just brandish one at them and they will gallop away."

"But why are we doing this?"

"George, it is not like you to be so thickheaded. We are doing this to impress Cecily, of course. She has been longing for an adventure and when she sees how brave you are she cannot help but fall head over ears in love with you."

George's face took on a mulish look. "I won't do it."

"What do you mean you won't do it," snapped Adriana.

"I'll not win Cecily by trickery. She must love me for myself. Besides, if she were to find out this was all an act, a pretty coward I should look."

"Well, you must do it. For imagine what a silly bunch of fools the rest of us will look if you do not."

Elizabeth had gone to the door and peeped out. "She's coming," she whispered, and opening the door stepped out into the hall. "I for one can hardly wait till we get to your aunt's for I am famished," she said.

"Yes. I, too," said Adriana, sweeping past her cousin. "Thank you, Cecily. Come along, George."

George glowered at his cousin's back but obediently followed her out the door.

The party arrived at Aunt Mary's safely. In spite of the absence of two of its members it didn't turn out to be as boring as Cecily had feared. Aunt Mary fussed over her and flattered her, and after dinner George, who had drunk a little too much wine with his dinner and lingered too long over his after-dinner brandy, kept them all highly amused by doing imitations of various barnyard animals. Then they tried their hands at conundrums, quitting only when Aunt Mary began to nod over her teacup.

Adriana had been watching the clock on the mantel and judged it time to leave. So after many thanks on their part and protestations on the part of their hostess, who claimed she was not a bit tired and couldn't understand why they must rush off, George and his ladies climbed into the coach and headed down the tree-lined drive and out into the night.

George had seemed perfectly relaxed at dinner. But he appeared more and more nervous as their carriage threaded its way down the country lanes. He could not seem to concentrate on his companions' conversation, his attention drawn to something out the carriage window.

Cecily looked out the window but could see nothing other than the dark shapes of moonlit trees. "What are you looking at?" she finally asked him.

George jumped. "Me? Oh, nothing. What could I possibly be looking at?"

"That is what I am wondering," said Cecily. "You keep looking out the window as if you expect to see highwaymen riding down on us at any minute."

"Highwaymen?" George's voice cracked from the strain. "Don't be silly."

"It is said Hounslow Heath was once a very dangerous place for travelers," said Cecily. "We could meet up with them, you know," she added with grisly relish. "And with no outriders we would be an easy target."

"That is highly unlikely," said Elizabeth. "We are more likely to encounter fog than robbers."

"You never know," said Cecily hopefully.

At that moment the sound of a gun made the three occupants inside the coach jump. "We are slowing down!" cried Cecily.

On top of the coach John nudged Samson the coachman. "There's only one," he said.

"Thought you said there'd be two," said Samson.

"So I did," muttered John. "But that's his lordship's bay, I'll swear. Don't shoot."

The lone horseman stopped his thundering horse next to the coach. The powerful animal reared and whinnied.

"Drop the noise boxes, gents," he commanded, motioning with his pistol.

Samson and John obeyed and tossed their guns onto the ground.

The man walked his horse to the carriage door, leaned over and opened it, and with a bow gestured the occupants out. Adriana and Elizabeth alighted first and seeing only one robber exchanged terrified looks. Next came Cecily, wide-eyed with trembling lips. She hesitated in the doorway and at the sight of the man gave a sob.

He pulled his scarf up higher over his face. "All the way out, missy," he said, motioning with his pistol.

Cecily tumbled out and landed next to Elizabeth, who put a protective arm around her.

George meanwhile had grabbed a pistol and came out hand first, waving it in all directions. It was neatly knocked out of his hand and fell with a thud onto the dirt. "Now come out nice, sir, or I'll have to put a hole in you, and the ladies wouldn't like to see such an awful sight," warned their attacker.

George came down, highly incensed at the unnecessary roughness his cousin was showing. And where was Lord Raine? Perhaps he and Wallingford had thought it would look more realistic if George chased away one villain instead of two. He must be hidden somewhere waiting for Wallingford to return. "Come down off that horse, you coward, and I'll teach you a lesson," declared George, warming to his part.

The highwayman laughed from behind his scarf. "What a brave fellow we have here."

"You scoundrel, come down and fight like a man!"

"George," said Adriana.

"I'll ram that pistol down your throat!"

"George—"

"I'll teach you what happens to lazy cowards who prey on defenseless travelers. I'll—"

"George! Do be quiet at once!" commanded Adriana.

"The lady is giving you good advice," the man said. "Best listen to it. Now, if you would all be so kind as to hand over your geegaws . . . I should hate to blow a hole in your protector's heart, but I will if I must."

The ladies began to unclasp their necklaces with shaking hands.

"You villain," hissed George. With that he made a lunge for the horseman, who leveled his pistol at George.

Adriana grabbed George's coat and pulled, then shut her eyes, unable to watch.

"Listen!" cried Elizabeth. "Someone is coming!" The sound of galloping horses was faint but unmistakable.

The highwayman had obviously heard the approaching riders, too. He jerked his horse's reins and sidled closer. "Hand 'em over—now!" he barked. The ladies deposited their jewels in his outstretched hand. Then he spurred his horse and galloped off.

Elizabeth sat down on the ground as if her legs had suddenly given way. Adriana leaned against the coach and Cecily ran into George's arms and burst into tears.

The sound of approaching riders grew louder and George suddenly realized how very vulnerable they were with their carriage standing still and all of them outside it. "Quickly," he ordered, "into the carriage."

"Oh, no, not more highwaymen!" squeaked Cecily, clinging to George.

George pried her loose and propelled her up the steps. As Adriana scrambled in he dragged Elizabeth from the ground and scooped up the pistol from where it lay, hoping he'd have time to load it.

George had barely gotten his ladies back inside and

ordered their coachman to make haste when they were overtaken by two riders, their hats pulled down and scarves covering the lower part of their faces. "Stand and deliver!" yelled the one on the big bay.

Again the carriage door was opened and its occupants spilled out. "You are a little late, sir," snapped Adriana. "We have already been robbed."

"You what?" exclaimed Wallingford, his scarf falling from his face.

"Bess, are you all right?" asked the other highwayman, jumping from his horse and rushing to Elizabeth's side.

George's mouth fell open. "W-Wallingford?" he stammered. "Then who was . . . ? Oh, my God." His legs buckled under him and he collapsed onto the carriage step.

• 10 •

WALLINGFORD JUMPED FROM his horse and rushed to his wife, more from instinct than because she looked in need of comfort. On the contrary, his lady looked very perturbed. "Are you all right?" he asked, putting an arm around her.

Adriana indicated her bare neck. "I am, as you can see, much lighter than I was when I set out this evening. What happened to you?"

"Charles's horse threw a shoe."

Cecily had, until now, stood dumbfounded, staring from one couple to another. "This was all a trick?" she asked.

The faces of her companions turned varying shades of red. No one seemed able to speak. Even Adriana, who was never at a loss for words, stood tongue-tied. She looked hopefully at her husband. But he suddenly became fully occupied with the task of brushing dust from the toe of his boot. The question hung unanswered, the two men on the box appearing almost as interested in the answer as Cecily.

No one of his acquaintance would ever accuse Lord Wallingford of being a coward. But looking at those flashing violet eyes would be enough to make anyone's blood run cold. So he did what any other sensible man would have done. "Adriana will explain it to you," he told his cousin as he got her back inside the carriage. His wife directed a reproachful look at him as she followed the others into the carriage. Wallingford closed the door with more force than was necessary and remounted to ride postilion.

His fellow bandit, still wearing a guilty flush, let out a low whistle. "I must say," he said in a whisper, "I'm glad we are out here and not in there. Poor George."

Poor George, indeed. He sat miserable and quiet as Cecily's recriminations ricocheted around his ears.

"Cecily, if you would please stop this carrying on we will endeavor to explain things to you," said Adriana. "You must not blame poor George, or Gerald and Charles. This was my idea."

"And mine," put in Elizabeth.

Cecily's mouth flew open, but before she could say anything Adriana hurried on. "I thought you would find it exciting to be waylaid by highwaymen, so we arranged this little, er, performance for you tonight. Of course, we never dreamed Charles's horse would cast a shoe and delay our husbands. And we certainly never dreamed we would be waylaid by a real highwayman. Thank God we had George with us," she said, smiling encouragingly at her cousin. "When did you first realize our attacker was not Gerald or Charles?" she asked innocently.

There it was. George's chance to appear a hero in Cecily's eyes. He could still feel the pleasant sensation of holding her trembling little body in his arms. She had finally seen him as the strong and courageous man he knew he was deep down inside. She had rushed to him for comfort. Thanks to Adriana's fast thinking she would always see him in a new light—if he would only accept the kind deception his cousin offered him. But he couldn't. He knew he had thought the robber was Wallingford, and he knew Adriana knew it also. Elizabeth, too, most likely. He would not hide behind a woman's skirts, even though he would rather die than have Cecily think worse of him than she already did. He took a deep breath, then said, "To be honest, Cousin, I thought the man to be your husband. Had I known who he really was, I would never have so foolishly risked all our lives."

Cecily's face, which had begun to glow, fell. She looked at George in disgust. "Then you did not really stand up to him. And you knew about this trick also!"

"He only found out about it just before we left," put in Adriana. "We had to tell him at the last minute for fear he would do something rash and mistakenly shoot Gerald or Charles."

Cecily's nerves had been stretched to the breaking point. She suddenly remembered that her neck and ears were missing some very pretty amethysts, and she began to cry in earnest. "This has been the worst night of my life," she wailed. "Mama would be horrified."

If Cecily had thought to verbally punish her cousin's wife, she much mistook the matter. Bad as she felt, Adriana would never be one to let a young lady three years her junior get the best of her. "Yes," she agreed. "She would probably order you home immediately if she were to hear what a havey cavey set you have fallen in with." Adriana sighed. "It all seemed so harmless. Such careful planning. Who would have thought such an unfortunate incident as Charles's horse throwing a shoe would lead us into a dangerous adventure. I vow no one else has had such an experience this Season."

Cecily sniffed and stared out the window and her two female companions shared a conspiratorial smile.

George was oblivious to everything going on around him. He sat morosely fingering his cousin's pistol and wishing it was loaded.

When the travelers finally returned home there was great speculation belowstairs about the peculiar prank the master had played on his cousin. It was agreed that there was truly no understanding the upper classes. "Too much inbreeding," Samson said to Cook. "That's what it is. It ain't good in horses and it ain't good in people."

Meanwhile, abovestairs a tired and grumpy Cecily was turned over to her maid, and Adriana went along to her own bedchamber, where she bid her maid to make haste with her toilet. "I am fagged to death and I would as lief be done and into bed quickly," she said.

Her maid was quick, but not quick enough, and Adriana wasn't able to gain her bed and feign sleep before her lord came to her. One look at his face told her their interview would not be a pleasant one. Obviously, the ride home had given her husband plenty of time to reflect on how ill-used he had been. Her maid saw trouble coming, too, and beat a hasty retreat.

Adriana padded over to her bed and took refuge among the pillows. Wallingford followed her across the room and stood sternly regarding her. He looked so very big standing next to her bed. One could not help but feel at a disadvantage when one's husband was towering over her like that. In spite of her nervousness she couldn't help wondering if this was what people meant when they spoke of someone being in a towering rage. She bit her lip and stared at her husband's knees.

"This was by far the most foolish, stupid thing I have ever done in my life. Do you realize, madam, what your little scheme could have cost? And do you see now why I did not want you to do such a thing? Why *I* did not want to do such a thing? Your cousin could have been killed."

Adriana judged it best not to tell him that her cousin *had* almost been killed. She bit her lip.

"And what if this gets out?" he continued. "Charles and I will certainly look like a fine pair of villains, leaving our wives at the mercy of thieves and rogues. Bah! I am disgusted with myself."

Adriana twisted the corner of her pegnoir and ventured a peep at her irate husband.

Wallingford looked at her and ran a hand through his hair. He shook his head and smiled. "I said I am disgusted with myself, not you, you goose." He sat down on the bed next to her. "I know that although your judgment was clouded, your motives were pure as new fallen snow, my love. You only wanted to help. And I must admit that if a real highwayman had not stumbled into the middle of our farce all would have ended well. But what took place is exactly the sort of thing I was worried might occur. What do you think would have become of all of you if Charles and I had been further delayed by even so much as a few moments. Really, love, I cannot have you embroiling us in these crazy schemes. I . . ." Adriana was now crying lustily. "There now," said Wallingford, taking her in his arms. "It is all right. Ssh." He kissed her hair and then her cheek. Her pegnoir had slipped, exposing a soft shoulder, and he kissed that, too. "Oh, never mind. We shan't talk of it anymore." he whispered.

Adriana's tears magically disappeared and she gave one final sniff. "Thank you, Gerald. I have learned my lesson. Truly, I have. From this moment on George is on his own. I'll not interfere between him and Cecily anymore. I promise you that."

"And I meant it," she insisted to Elizabeth the next morning as they sat in Adriana's drawing room.

"I am sure Cecily, at least, will thank you for that," said Elizabeth. "And speaking of Cecily, where is she?"

"She is in her bedroom, sulking."

"Is she going to write her mama?"

Adriana made a face. "Empty threats. You know Cecily would rather die than go home before her London Season is over. And even though she pretends to have been unkindly used, I think she is secretly relishing the whole thing. Unfortunately, she still sees George's participation in our scheme in a highly unfavorable light."

Elizabeth shook her head in sympathy and Adriana continued. "I reminded her that he had, after all, stood up to a real highwayman, but she said that did not signify, for he had thought the man was Gerald."

"Well!" declared Elizabeth. "And I suppose it took no courage to admit his part in the whole affair. He could have, after all, pretended to have discovered the man was truly a highwayman. And she would have never known otherwise."

"So I told her," said Adriana. "In fact, it may not have been wise, but I told her the reason behind the escapade and of George's reluctance to cooperate. But that did not help. She may be impressed by all the trouble we went to on her behalf, but as for George, her opinion of him has definitely sunk." Adriana sighed. "Well, there's an end to it. I am sure George is once again packing his things. And I must say I do not blame him."

"It is a pity you said you would not interfere," said Elizabeth, looking innocently at the ceiling.

Adriana looked suspiciously at her cousin. "Yes," she said slowly, "it is."

"Of course, *I* made no such promise."

"Do you have an idea?" asked Adriana hopefully.

Elizabeth nodded. "I plan to make a morning call on Miss Courtland. Would you care to accompany me?"

"I suppose there could be no harm in accompanying you on a morning call," said Adriana slowly. "And I must admit you have now aroused my curiosity. Of course, this scheme, whatever it is, is entirely yours, so Gerald could hardly accuse *me* of interfering."

"Oh, he certainly couldn't!" agreed Elizabeth.

"Very well," said Adriana. "Tell me what *you* are planning."

· 11 ·

MISS COURTLAND'S BUTLER informed the two ladies that his mistress was presently engaged and unable to receive callers. Adriana gave him her card and said, "Please take this to Miss Courtland and tell her we have urgent business that cannot wait."

The butler obeyed and disappeared. He returned a few minutes later and conducted the ladies to an elegant drawing room, decorated in shades of pale green and gold. Although the sun was out there was enough of a chill in the spring morning to warrant the cheerful fire burning in the fireplace.

Standing next to the mantel, looking slightly embarrassed, stood the honorable Mr. Eagan, and sitting on a dainty Hepplewhite chair, wearing a pea green morning gown, green kid slippers, and a becoming flush which could have nothing to do with the fire burning nearby, sat Miss Kate Courtland.

"Oh, I can see we have indeed come at an inopportune time," said Elizabeth penitently.

"Oh, no," said Kate graciously, rising from her chair. "But if you have something urgent to discuss, perhaps we should do so quickly, as I imagine Mama will be here any minute. She knew Albert was calling on Papa this morning."

"Our heartfelt congratulations to you both," said Adriana. "You make a prodigious fine pair."

Albert came to Kate's side and put a proprietorial hand on his newly affianced bride's shoulder. "Yes, I think we do," he said with a proud smile.

"But do be seated and tell us what brings you here," said Kate. "I hope nothing is amiss with Cecily."

"There is nothing amiss with Cecily," said Elizabeth. "It is Adriana's cousin, George, we are worried about. I do not think we are disclosing a secret by saying George has formed a tendre for Cecily."

Kate sighed. "It is a sad thing, for she does not appreciate him at all. She has set her sights on a fortune and a title—an earl at the least."

Adriana made a face. "She has no need of a fortune," she said. "And George does inherit a title."

"He won't be an earl," Elizabeth reminded her. She turned again to Kate. "But what Cecily wants and what is best for her we feel are two entirely different things. The fact is, Adriana and I are both convinced George would be perfect for Cecily. And we feel she would realize that . . . with just a little help."

"We want to help, don't we, Albert?" said Kate, turning to her beloved.

"Of course," said Albert. "But I don't know what more we can do. I already taught him the mathematical."

Adriana suppressed a smile.

"You are a good friend," replied Elizabeth seriously. "But I fear it will take even more than a well-tied cravat for George to win Cecily at this point. We feel that if Cecily saw George was special in someone else's eyes she might realize what a treasure he is and want him for herself."

"Oh, that is an excellent idea!" exclaimed Kate. "Who are you going to get to help George make Cecily jealous?"

"We thought it should be someone beautiful," said Elizabeth. "It would hardly impress Cecily if a plain girl was attracted to George. And we felt it should be someone Cecily knows, someone who's opinion she respects."

"And," put in Adriana, "it must be someone George knows and with whom he would be comfortable."

"To be frank," said Elizabeth, "we had hoped to enlist your help, Miss Courtland."

Albert had moved to a nearby chair and sat lounging comfortably in it, nodding his head in agreement and swinging his quizzing glass. With this last statement he sat bolt upright, his eyes popping out. "What?" he sputtered. "Kate cannot chase after George. She's just promised to marry me!"

"Yes," Elizabeth said, nodding sadly. "I am afraid our timing is deplorable. And we could hardly ask you and Miss Courtland to postpone your happiness by helping us. It is a pity, though. I don't know what we shall do now, for this was quite our last hope. Ah, well. George will return to his family and forget Cecily . . . someday. Of course, it will be hard on him for a while, but that cannot be helped. And I suppose Cecily will marry a man with a title and fortune who does not love her as deeply as George does. She will grow to be a lonely old woman and look back on this time of her life with deep regret. But then, she won't be the first woman to choose unwisely and pay for it the rest of her life."

Kate's eyes filled with tears. She looked at Albert. "Do you not think we should help?"

"Well, of course I'd like to help, but . . ." Albert began.

"Could we not postpone announcing our engagement for just a little while?"

"How long?" asked Albert suspiciously.

"Oh, no more than a fortnight," Adriana assured him. "If this plan has not worked by then it never will."

Albert did not look enthusiastic. "What will your parents say?" he asked Kate. "They know I have come here today to propose to you."

Kate considered this for a moment. "I shall tell them I am not yet sure of my heart and have asked you to give me a little time to consider before giving you an answer."

"Well," said Albert hesitantly.

"Surely you want your friend to find the same happiness we have found," prodded Kate.

"Of course," Albert said. He sat silent for a moment, all three women watching him with bated breath. "You promise you won't fall in love with him?" he said to Kate.

"Albert!"

"Oh, very well. But only for two weeks," Albert said firmly.

George was not much easier to talk into this latest farce than Albert had been. When his friend arrived at his apartments he found George busily packing. "Here now, what's all this?" asked Albert, looking at the collection of cravats, shirts, and breeches George's valet was carefully folding and stowing in a shiny new trunk.

"I am leaving. London no longer interests me," said George. "I am going back home where I belong."

"Well, you can't," said Albert firmly. He turned to George's valet. "Take those clothes out of that trunk. Here, leave this mess and come find me something to drink," he said, taking George by the arm and propelling him from the bedroom, shutting the door firmly behind them. "What has happened between you and Miss Hammond this time?"

George stiffened. He poured his friend a drink and coldly replied, "Miss Hammond has nothing to do with my decision to leave."

"Cut line," snapped Albert. "This is me, Albert, you are talking to. Anyway, if you don't want to tell me that's fine, but you must stay in town a little longer before admitting defeat. We have a plan."

"We? Who is 'we'? Oh, no!" George fell into a chair, clapped his head between his hands and rested his elbows on his knees. "Don't tell me my cousin has had yet another brilliant idea."

"Actually, I think it was her sister-in-law," said Albert.

"Yet another person takes a hand at writing the play," George moaned. "I am beginning to feel like a puppet."

"Well, do you want to win the girl or not?" asked Albert reasonably.

"Of course I do," said George. "But a courtship should be a thing between two people. There is an entire crowd involved with mine."

Albert scratched his head. "I see what you mean," he said. "But look, this really is a rather good idea. Don't you at least want to hear it?"

"I suppose," said George, resignedly slumping against his chair.

Albert related the ladies' plan, carefully ticking off on his fingers all the reasons he had been instructed to give as to why this latest idea would work.

George rubbed his chin thoughtfully. "It could work. At any rate I have nothing to lose."

"Yes, well, just see to it that you remember Kate is only pretending an interest in you," cautioned Albert.

George gave his friend a wounded look. "Of course. I know you are interested in Kate yourself."

"I am more than that," declared Albert. "I am engaged to the lady."

"No! Why, you never told me you were going to ask her to marry you."

"Didn't know it myself," said Albert.

"When did this happen?"

"Just this morning. And I can tell you it took all your cousin's powers of persuasion to talk me into postponing sending our announcement to the *Gazette*." George looked troubled but Albert smiled and said simply, "You are my closest friend. It is the least I could do to help you."

George was deeply moved. "Here!" he declared, jumping from his chair and grabbing the wine decanter from its silver tray. He poured his friend and himself a glass. "A toast. To your happiness."

"To *our* happiness," Albert corrected him.

The following week at the Eversham's masked ball Cecily was relieved to see that the tall, skinny figure in the scarlet domino stayed far away from her. She was dressed as the goddess Diana, her gown a diaphonous creation in lavender, a tiny silver arrow in her hand and a pearl tiara in her hair. Her most ardent admirer was a dashing Elizabethan pirate, who's mask had not fooled her for a moment. Lord Spenser had been very attentive, and she told him he made a terribly handsome pirate, if not a terrifying one. He had assured her he had no desire to terrify her, only all her other suitors. Of course, they were not terrified either, and whenever she was not dancing she had at least two men by her side all night.

It was truly an evening any young lady would record in her journal as a complete success. Yet, as Cecily watched the tall, scarlet domino claim yet another dance with a Helen of Troy, an irritation began growing at the back of her mind that prevented the evening from falling into that category. The real Helen of Troy had golden curls, Cecily thought, looking critically at this fair Helen's auburn ones. Where was Kate's mama? Was she not watching how many times her daughter danced with the same man? Well, who cared? If Kate wanted to throw herself away on a cowardly sneak that was her affair. And George was welcome to her. But it was certainly rude of him to ignore her for Kate all evening. He could at least say hello to her, no matter how infatuated he was with the Helen with the wrong-colored curls.

There was no more time to watch the red domino and his Helen, for Lord Spenser had arrived to claim his dance. "I have come to pirate you away," he said as he swept her onto the dance floor.

Cecily laughed at this sally and told his lordship he was truly brilliant.

Across the room the red domino's mouth sadly drooped as he watched Lord Spenser twirling his vision in lavender. She looked so beautiful, so soft, so . . . .

"Mr. Atherby, you must pretend to be enjoying yourself," prodded his partner.

"Oh, beg pardon," said George humbly.

"I am not insulted," laughed Kate, "but if you wish to make Cecily jealous you must give a more convincing performance than you are right now."

"It all seems rather hopeless," said George sadly.

His companion had seen the surreptitious looks thrown their way that evening, and she was not sure the situation was as hopeless as George thought it. Cecily was laughing a little too much, and she looked just a little too determined in her flirtations. Kate suspected she and George were not the only actors at the ball that night. Could it be her friend's eyes were turning a little green? "Do not despair," she told George. "I think Cecily cares for you more than she wants to admit."

"Do you really think so?" asked George, suddenly animated.

Kate shook her head at him and giggled. "Such sudden liveliness, sir. I can see that if I want you to show a convincing interest in me I shall have to take care to always talk of Cecily when we are together." George blushed and she laughed at him.

Across the room Cecily peeped around Lord Spenser's arm and saw this interchange. What, she wondered, did Kate see in George Atherby? And, for that matter, what did George see in Kate? She wasn't *that* beautiful. What did Kate have that she, Cecily, didn't have more of? Why stop pursuing the Season's reigning beauty to dangle after a female who was merely lovely? George's eyes had once followed her wherever she went. Now he was completely unaware of her. How could her faithless admirer switch loyalties like this?

"Are you all right, Miss Hammond?" asked Lord Spenser, observing the scowl on his partner's face.

"I am fine," declared Cecily. "There is nothing wrong with me—nothing whatsoever!"

Lord Spenser might have questioned this statement if Cecily hadn't followed it with one of her famous brilliant smiles and a compliment on his dancing—enough to convince him that there could be nothing wrong with her after all.

The music slowed to a stop and the dancers fanned out to all corners of the room. Cecily watched the scarlet domino lead Helen of Troy out a pair of French doors and onto the balcony, and her eyes narrowed behind her mask. It was no business of hers if Kate wished to make herself appear fast. And she had no intention of spying on her and George. But she was feeling quite warm. It was so terribly close in this room she was sure she would faint. Cecily unfurled her fan with a flourish and informed Lord Spenser she absolutely must have a breath of fresh air. There was, after all, no law against more than two people standing on a balcony at the same time.

Kate saw Cecily and her captive pirate descending on them before George did and smiled. "Do not look," she said, "but Cecily appears to feel the need of some air." Kate chuckled. "I must say, Mr. Atherby, I find it rather a pleasant sensation, this ability to make the beautiful Cecily Hammond jealous. I shall have to thank your cousin and Lady Elizabeth next time I see them for allowing me to take part in a harmless deception that not only will give you the woman of your dreams, but which is giving me an increasingly higher opinion of myself. Oh, they are almost upon us. Pray, do not show anything more than a friendly interest in Cecily or our evening's work will have been for naught!" And with this Kate's expression changed from one of simple friendliness to rapt adoration. "How ever did you come to know so much about the constellations, Mr. Atherby?" she gushed.

George stumbled over his reply, but the knowledge Cecily was approaching spurred him on and he rose to the part, showing a calm he was far from feeling.

"I see we are not the only ones in need of fresh air," said a gay voice behind them.

George turned to see Cecily with her hand resting gently on Lord Spenser's arm. It had been hard enough to watch her dancing with Spenser. Must he now bring her out here and flaunt his prize under George's nose? An angry flush spread across his face. He glowered at Lord Spenser, whose pirate costume George found most appropriate. The only reason, thought George irrationally, that Spenser had Cecily now was because he had been underhanded enough to pilfer another man's words of love and use them to impress an innocent and trusting female. George ground his teeth.

"Good evening, Lord Spenser," said Kate gaily, trying to

compensate for her companion's sudden silence and downturned mouth. "It is Lord Spenser I see beneath those pirate rags, is it not?"

"Aye," laughed Lord Spenser, obviously enjoying his moment of triumph. "And I have captured the season's most beautiful prize. Wouldn't you agree, Atherby? It is Atherby under that cape, isn't it? I recognized the legs."

George's face was deepening to an alarming shade of red and Kate suddenly became very chilly. "I think we had best go in," she said. "It is getting rather cold out here."

"As you wish," said George. "I must say," he continued, "the air doesn't seem as fresh as it was a few minutes ago."

Lord Spenser's chin went up a few more notches and Cecily's eyes widened in shock. "Well!" she exclaimed as George and Kate went back into the ballroom. "How very churlish. He said not a word to me. He did not even compliment me on my gown."

Lord Spenser, obviously preoccupied, merely grunted, and suddenly Cecily wondered what was supposed to be so wonderful about a masked ball, anyway?

• 12 •

GEORGE LEFT THE Eversham's ball in the blackest of moods. Kate had tried, but had been unable to convince him that his beloved Cecily was really interested in him. Interested? Ha! It was not his arm on which that dainty hand had rested. And it was not at him that those beautiful violet eyes had gazed. It was Lord Spenser, the man of no principles, who held Cecily's heart.

George and Albert found their way to Brooks's after the ball and settled in with a pack of cards and a decanter of port. As the game progressed and the level of the dark, red liquid in the decanter dropped, George's face took on an increasingly grim look in spite of the fact that he was winning. When Lord Spenser strolled into the room George's eyebrows knit together and a recognizable growl was heard by his companion.

Albert followed his friend's angry gaze and cleared his throat. "I say, perhaps we should call it a night, eh?"

George ignored Albert's suggestion, watching Lord Spenser's approach with a venomous look. "Look at him," he sneered. "The scoundrel has no conscience to trouble him."

Albert gulped and again suggested they leave.

Lord Spenser had caught sight of George and returned his look with one of haughty disdain. George's glare did nothing to halt his progress. He continued to thread his way past the various tables and chairs scattered about the card room. As he approached their table, George shuffled the cards and said conversationally, "It is a shame such a select club extends membership to scoundrels and thieves. If I had known how indiscriminating they were, I doubt I would have joined."

Lord Spenser froze next to their table. "Who were you calling a thief, Atherby?"

"There is no one here but you whom I know for one," replied George calmly.

Lord Spenser's face took on a deep flush and his eyes narrowed to slits. He slammed both hands down on the table. "Damn your insolent eyes, Atherby! You'll take that back or regret it."

George jumped from his chair, his face red with anger and too much wine. "We both know I would be lying if I did," he snarled. "I tell you to your face, sir, you are a thief. You take credit for another man's work. Is that the only way you can win a woman?"

The remark was barely out of George's mouth when Lord Spenser struck him. "I will have satisfaction, sir," Spenser growled. He turned to his companion. "Rawley?"

Lord Rawley nodded. "Of course," he murmured.

"Albert, will you second me?" asked George between clenched teeth.

"Certainly," said Albert. "Call on you tomorrow, old fellow," he said to the other second, who moved on with Lord Spenser. Albert collapsed into his chair and George sunk into his, a stunned expression on his face. "Do you wish to leave this world at an early age?" hissed Albert. "Spenser is a crack shot."

"So am I," replied George. Albert looked doubtful. "Well, I'm not bad," he amended.

"Not bad will not help you in a duel. Spenser is a regular

at Manton's. He could shoot a fly from your head without removing a single hair if he had a mind to. What the devil were you thinking of?"

George ran a distracted hand through his hair. "I don't know. I was just so angry. He stole my poem. And he is going to get Cecily!"

"He is now," said Albert. "You'll hardly be able to stop him from the grave."

A mulish look came over George. "I don't think Spenser should be allowed to get away with what he did."

"Chances are he wouldn't have. He'd have been found out eventually. You should have let me tell her you wrote the poem." Albert was silent awhile, lost in thought. "I don't understand what you are so devilish mad about," he said finally. "Granted, it was a rotten piece of luck, but it ain't as if Spenser made a personal assault on you."

"It was a personal assault!" George declared.

"Curse it all, Atherby!" Albert hiccuped and shook his head. "He probably didn't even know it was you who wrote that poem." George looked at his friend uncomprehendingly and Albert continued. "Don't you remember? He just picked up the paper and handed it to Miss Hammond. It ain't his fault she thought he wrote it. A silly clunch he would have looked if he'd done anything but what he did."

George suddenly looked deflated. "You're right." He sighed. "*I* am the silly clunch. I deserve to be shot for being so stupid."

Albert shrugged. "Perhaps Spenser will miss," he said without conviction.

George slept poorly that night. Lord Spenser and Cecily danced in his dreams—literally. She smiled up at Lord Spenser as he recited poetry to her—George's poetry. And George was powerless to stop it, for in his dream he was a wraith. And he found being a ghost most unpleasant. The icy fingers of death moved over him and made him cold, so very cold. He awoke to find he had tossed off all his blankets. Shivering, he left the dubious comforts of his bed in search of a late breakfast. He was cutting into a thick slice of ham when Alfred arrived. George found himself suddenly not very hungry. "Well?" he asked, laying down his knife and fork.

"It is set for tomorrow. Seven o'clock at Kensington Gardens."

George had rather hoped for some place a little more solitary and said so.

"Kensington Gardens at seven in the morning will be plenty solitary," Albert assured him. "Spenser and Rawley will be there ahead of us to go over the ground and will, of course, bring the physician."

George gulped and nodded stoically. Oh, Cecily, he thought. I am doing this all for you and you do not even care.

If Cecily had been able to read George's melancholy thoughts, she would have assured him that, indeed, she did not care. All the way home from the ball and the next morning as well she continued to tell herself that her once ardent admirer's loss of interest didn't bother her. When Adriana remarked on how little they had seen of George the last few days, Cecily answered with studied nonchalance, "He seems to have developed a fast friendship with Miss Courtland."

"You mean your friend Kate?" asked Adriana, making a gleeful mental note of the formal use Cecily made of her best friend's name.

Cecily tied the ribbons on her new bonnet and studied its effect in the drawing-room mirror. "Yes, and I am sure I wish them both well. Although I must say I consider it rather shabby of Kate to throw over poor Mr. Eagan for someone else's admirer. And why she should toss aside a future viscount for someone who will only be a baronet is more than I can fathom."

"Perhaps she realized there is more to a man than his title," said Adriana innocently.

Cecily blushed. "Well, I am sure I realize that, too," she said. "But a girl must be practical. And besides, there was nothing wrong with the man she had. To take a friend's—" Cecily stopped herself. "I am sure the way Miss Courtland behaves is none of my affair."

"And none of mine, either," agreed Adriana, smiling to herself. "You look very fetching in that new bonnet. I am sure Lord Spenser will appreciate it when he takes you driving."

Cecily brightened at the mention of the ever faithful Lord Spenser. *His* loyalties did not waver. Or did they? Adriana had barely finished speaking when the message from Lord Spenser arrived. Cecily read it and her mouth turned down in a pout.

"What does he say?" asked Adriana.

"He says something very urgent has come up and he will be unable to take me driving this afternoon. He asks me to allow him to do so next Monday instead. Whatever can have happened to make him wish to postpone our drive?" Cecily finished in irritation.

"I am sure whatever it is, it is something important. A gentleman would hardly cancel an engagement unless something terribly important had come up," said Adriana.

Something important had indeed come up—target practice! Lord Spenser was an excellent marksman, but like any other man who prided himself on his skill, he believed in dedicating time and effort to keeping that skill sharp. And watching his Lordship's face that afternoon as he carefully aimed his pistol and squeezed the trigger, one would quickly get the impression that he wanted his skills especially sharp for the next morning. Perhaps a guilty conscience was what had made Atherby's insult sting so terribly, more than his lordship's friends could know. They only knew Atherby was an insolent fellow who should be taken down a peg or two, and told his lordship so. "He will be," said Lord Spenser. Again, he raised his arm, fired, and shattered the bottle cork sitting twenty-five yards away.

George was also practicing that afternoon. But whereas his opponent was easily hitting his mark eight out of ten times, George's success rate was considerably lower. Albert watched his friend's efforts with a glum face. "Should've apologized," he muttered. George looked insulted and Albert blushed. "Sorry," he said. "Of course you can't. After all, it was your poem. Of course, Spenser didn't know that," he continued fairly. "He probably does now." Albert was silent a moment, deep in thought. George watched him, hoping he would come up with a way to stop the upcoming duel. "Well," said Albert finally, "the fellow is curst high in the instep anyway and he should be taught a lesson."

George sighed. "It probably won't be me who teaches him." He turned to his friend. "Look, old fellow. If anything should . . ." George swallowed hard and continued bravely on, ". . . happen to me, will you tell Cecily the truth about the poem?"

Albert nodded solemnly and prayed silently that the world would end before the next sunrise.

Nothing happened to prevent the sun from rising the next morning, and even the blanket of fog that hung over London couldn't hide the fact. George and Albert arrived at Kensington Gardens promptly at seven to find Lord Spenser and his second, Lord Rawley already there along with the surgeon.

The damp fog swirled around George as he stepped down

from Albert's curricle and he shivered, though whether from the cold or an unpleasant feeling of doom he couldn't be sure.

Rawley came up to greet them, carrying a mahogany box with a brass handle. George looked at it and shivered again. "We've already gone over the field," Rawley said cheerfully. He opened the box with loving care and displayed its contents. "Look at these."

George forced himself to look inside the velvet-lined case. There, nestled in its contoured recesses, lay two very serviceable-looking dueling pistols. No frivolous display pieces, these. They were well crafted and designed for the serious duelist. There was no silver or gold inlay on these lethal weapons, nothing which could catch the sun and cause a momentary, fatal, glare. There was checkering, on the butt of the guns, but no decoration which might in the least way impair the shooter's hold.

"French," said Rawley. "Boutet himself supervised the making of 'em. Beauties, ain't they? Perfectly balanced. And they've got a hair-trigger."

George knew about hair-triggers. If a duelist wasn't careful he could shoot off his foot before he even had a chance to raise his pistol. George's mouth felt dry and he swallowed hard. His heart was thumping wildly, but he compressed his lips in grim determination. He would have no one thinking him a coward.

While the principals stripped off their hats and coats and waistcoats, their seconds examined the pistols, then loaded and cocked them, and handed them to the principals.

George took his with a slightly shaking hand. He looked at Lord Spenser. The look he received in return was a haughty one. He glared at his enemy. He was going to teach the fellow a lesson or die trying. Die? George swallowed hard.

Lord Spenser's second was speaking. "It has been agreed that one round of fire will give satisfaction," he said. "Eagan, you will drop the handkerchief?"

Albert nodded solemnly and George and Lord Spenser retired to their respective positions. In the few seconds remaining before his dance with death, many thoughts whirled through George's mind. Twenty yards away from him stood his rival, the man who had stolen his poem and would, if allowed to live, end up with Cecily. For his underhanded dealings Lord Spenser truly deserved to die, didn't he? But if George shot and killed Lord Spenser, would Cecily ever forgive him? Most likely not. Best to merely wound the scoundrel. He would hit Spenser in the shoulder. That would teach him to run around picking up other men's love notes! George eyed his opponent and hoped he would be able even to hit him at all.

"Are you ready, gentlemen?" called Albert. The two men nodded and watched as Albert extended his arm. He released his hold on the handkerchief and it fluttered to the ground to the sound of gunfire. Lord Spenser dropped his arm and remained standing, a look of satisfaction on his face. George dropped his pistol, staggered backward and fell to the ground.

"Atherby!" cried Albert, and rushed to his side, the physician following.

George sat on the ground, frowning at his quickly reddening upper arm.

Albert, on seeing that his friend's wound was not a mortal one, covered his momentary emotional display by clapping George on his other arm. "Well done, old fellow," he said, smiling.

George gritted his teeth and smiled weakly. He looked at Lord Spenser shrugging himself carelessly back into his coat and frowned. "I didn't even wing him," he grumbled.

"Never mind that," said Albert. "Just be glad he did not kill you. He could have easily, y'know."

George looked thoughtfully across the field of honor at his rival. Yes, he could have. Why didn't he? Did Lord Spenser have a conscience, perhaps? Maybe he was more of a sport than George had given him credit for being.

"Good show," called Rawley gaily as the two men headed for their curricle.

George's arm hurt like the devil. He gritted his teeth. Lord Spenser was still alive and would most likely spend the next two weeks squiring Cecily around town while he nursed a very sore arm. Good show, indeed!

• 13 •

George's prediction had been correct. He didn't see Cecily for the next two weeks. But thanks to Albert he was aware of everything she did. Albert had seen her driving with Lord Spenser shortly after the duel. But not to worry, because she had also been out driving with Farley as well. She had also been at the Brindell's rout. Yes, Lord Spenser had been there, but he was not her only suitor. Evanston had stayed by her side most of the evening. And she had flirted a great deal with Sir Winston.

"Sir Winston! That old toad?"

Albert shrugged. "You know females. There's no understanding 'em. She seems to prefer Spenser, but he's far from having her all to himself."

George took comfort in his friend's observation. Until the next time he saw Albert. Cecily had waltzed with Lord Spenser three times at Lady Allistair's ball. And, yes, she had even gone in to supper with him. And Albert had seen her driving with him yesterday.

"That does it! I am going out," George announced.

"And what are you going to do, take her driving? You are in no shape to use that arm."

"Today is Tuesday. My cousin is usually at home on Tuesday afternoons. I will stop by for a visit." George bellowed for his valet, and Albert watched with misgivings as the man shaved George and assisted him in getting dressed.

George winced as his man finally helped him into his coat, and Albert shook his head. "Look at you. How the devil are you going to keep that wound a secret if you go out like this?"

"If anyone asks me, I'll just say I . . ." George stopped. What would he say? He chewed his lip thoughtfully. "I have it! I'll say I fell off my horse."

"Can't say that," said Albert. "Miss Hammond's seen you ride. She'd never believe it. Besides, that'll make you look a regular dolt."

"True," admitted George. "Well, then. I'll say I hurt it working out at Jackson's." Albert didn't look impressed with this excuse but could come up with nothing better, so George decided to stick with this story. "Besides," he added, "it ain't that noticeable that my arm is sore."

"Well, just sit still and don't move," Albert advised. "Oughta have let me told her what happened," he grumbled. "Then she would have found out who wrote the poem."

George shook his head. "I'd just look like a poor sport, and a poor shot."

Albert scratched his head. "I guess you're right," he said.

As Hastings ushered George into his cousin's drawing room he began to wonder if he shouldn't have taken his friend's advice and waited a little longer to see Cecily. The room was full of females. George swallowed nervously. It wasn't that he was afraid of women . . . in small numbers. But a drawing room full of them was enough to make any man want to turn tail and run.

It was too late for that, however, for Adriana was already calling a cheery welcome. She patted the chair next to her in invitation and George joined her. "Well, George, what have you been doing? We have not seen you this age and more. Have we, Cecily?"

Cecily sat nearby, a vision in a pale pink frock. "Oh, has George been gone?" she asked innocently. "I am afraid I had not even noticed his absence."

George took a piece of the poppy seed cake his cousin offered him and ground it between his teeth. Don't look like a cloddish oaf, he warned himself. Choose your words carefully. "I am sure you would not have noticed," he answered kindly. "How can a beautiful woman be expected to keep track of the comings and goings of all her admirers?"

"Oh, very prettily said!" exclaimed a generously curved woman in her early thirties sitting nearby. "Adriana, love, it seems to me I have not yet met this charming young man."

Cecily's eyes opened wide as the older woman exchanged her seat for one on the other side of George.

"Dear Lady Penelope," said Adriana with a laugh. "George is not at all your style. But if you promise to behave I shall introduce him."

"Oh, I promise to behave, but I can make no promises as to *how* I will behave," the young woman replied archly and batted her eyelashes at George.

George looked at her with his mouth agape. Of course she was too old for him, but it was flattering, nonetheless, to be noticed by a woman who, by any man's standards, would be considered a lovely armful. In addition to having a generously curved figure, the lady also boasted creamy, smooth skin, large blue eyes, and hair the color of spun gold. Her blond beauty was not quite a match for his cousin's—her nose was a little less finely chiseled than Adriana's, and her lips were a little too large. Nonetheless, she was a striking woman, and with Cecily's eyes boring into him George felt uncomfortably guilty for noticing.

"Lady Penelope Darcy, may I present my cousin, the honorable George Atherby? He is visiting London this Season."

"Indeed you may," purred Lady Penelope. George took the proffered hand, then was not sure what to do with it. Uncomfortably aware of Cecily's gaze, he blushingly kissed it.

Lady Penelope smiled dotingly on him and inquired politely if this was George's first visit to the metropolis.

With an effort he made the proper reply. Between the attentions of the beautiful Lady Penelope and the jealous glare of Cecily, he found he was having a great deal of trouble concentrating. His arm began to throb, and he wished he had stayed home.

Lady Penelope turned to Adriana. "I do believe if I had known you had imported such a delightful young man to town I would have come back from that stuffy old house party much sooner," she said.

Once again Cecily's eyes opened wide in astonishment, then narrowed. George squirmed.

"Lady Penelope," said Adriana sweetly. "Did you not say you had to leave us at half past?" She looked pointedly at the clock on the mantle.

Lady Penelope sighed. "I am now sorry I am pledged to my sister for the rest of the afternoon. Ah, well. Perhaps we will meet again, Mr. Atherby," she said, rising.

George rose and bowed over her hand and said the only polite thing he could say, which was that he hoped they would, and cringed inwardly as he felt Cecily's indignant gaze burning into his back. He watched Lady Penelope glide out the door and breathed a sigh of relief, as did most of the women in the room. Under cover of the general chatter, George relocated himself next to Cecily.

"Really, *Mr*. Atherby," said Cecily. "I never realized what a favorite with the ladies you were."

"Am I?" asked George. He looked meaningfully at Cecily.

She blushed and plucked at her skirt. "You certainly seem to be," she said. "Lady Penelope is obviously very taken with you."

For all his inexperience, George was one of those rare males who was smart enough to know the difference between a woman who was merely flirting and one who was smitten. "There is only one female whom I wish to have taken with me," he said, smiling down at Cecily.

It was hard to mistake his meaning, but Cecily seemed determined to do so. Surely her blush showed she had understood him, or did she just blush at her own boldness? "I have not seen either you or Kate much lately," she said, still too preoccupied with her gown to look at George.

Now what should he say? He had no idea what Kate had been up to. As for himself, he could hardly tell Cecily he had tried to shoot her wealthiest and most highly titled suitor and received a bullet in the arm and two weeks of bedrest for his trouble. He hedged. "I have been busy," he said.

"And has Kate been busy, also?"

How the devil should he know? "Er, yes. Most likely she has, too," he answered vaguely.

Cecily's eyes narrowed. "I see," she said, with a toss of her curls. "You must excuse me now. I do have other guests to see to." With that she moved from her chair, picked up the plate of dainty cakes and breads, and without offering George so much as a crumb, circulated with it among the other guests.

George frowned and rubbed his sore arm. It was definitely time to go home. He bid his hostess farewell and made good his escape. On his way out he met Lord Wallingford coming in. "Had enough petticoat company for one day?" asked his lordship.

George nodded.

"Why don't you join me in the library. I can offer you something a little more refreshing than tea."

George thanked his cousin-in-law and followed him into the book-lined room. It smelled of leather and snuff, a very refreshing smell after inhaling the overpowering mixture of favorite female fragrances.

Wallingford poured George a glass of Madeira and handed it to him. "How is your arm?" he asked.

"My arm?" George repeated stupidly. He felt a telltale blush creeping over his face and took a drink from his goblet. "Does Cecily know?" he asked finally.

Wallingford shook his head. "Neither of the ladies know." George let out a sigh of relief and Wallingford grinned at him. "I cannot say I blame you, but I do hope you are not going to make a habit of going about challenging crack shots like Spenser. I am sure if anything were to happen to you your cousin would blame me."

"I don't intend to make a habit of this," said George. "I have realized I am too much of a coward and far too fond of breathing to take up dueling as a hobby." George hesitated. "I suppose I am a laughingstock," he said, fingering his glass.

"On the contrary," said Wallingford, lowering himself into a wing-backed chair and crossing one booted leg over another. "Spenser has said you are a hotheaded, uppity fellow, but pluck to the bone. No one knows what the quarrel was about for Spenser will not say."

"I should guess he wouldn't," said George bitterly. "Oh, well, it is over and I am glad to be alive."

"You should be," said Wallingford. "I have seen your rival a few times at Manton's. If he had wanted to, Spenser could have put a bullet through your heart."

"He has more conscience than I had supposed," said George. He smiled at Wallingford. "Thank you for not telling Adriana."

"There are some things females don't understand," Wallingford said with a smile. "Speaking of females, how is my spoiled little cousin?"

George's smile disappeared. He shook his head. "I don't understand females," he complained.

Wallingford laughed. "Do you think there is a man alive who does?"

George didn't laugh. "I begin to think I shall never win her."

Wallingford was silent. "Go out and do something tonight that will take your mind off Cecily," he finally advised.

Albert came by George's lodgings that evening on his way to a cockfight to hear how George had fared. "Told you not to go," he said at the sight of his friend's long face.

George had already made great inroads on a decanter of port and he sniffed pitifully. "Should've listened to you," he said.

"Here now! I know what will make you feel better. Come with me to the Cock Pit Royal. It will do you good."

Alfred was right. George did feel much better once in the relaxing atmosphere of strictly male company. The Cock Pit Royal smelled of smoke and sweat and chickens, but that didn't bother George. Here a man could be himself. He could say whatever came into his head and not have to worry how it would be interpreted. He won forty guineas betting on a Red Pyle, then lost it again next battle. He laughed and joked and drank some more, fell on his wounded arm on the way home and set it to throbbing fiercely. Yes, it was altogether a satisfying evening!

Cecily's evening was anything but satisfying. Sir Winston had sent her some lovely violets ("to match your eyes"), which she had worn to yet another ball. Was there no end to the number of balls a reigning beauty must attend? Adriana's irritating cousin was conspicuous by his absence. Kate was there, but Cecily had no desire to talk to her traitorous friend, and managed to avoid her all evening. Even Lord Spenser was missing, making the affair especially flat. Cecily dutifully flirted with Sir Winston until the horrid creature she had met that afternoon came and stole him away. Really, was Lady Penelope's mission in life to take away all Cecily's suitors? Oh, where was George, anyway! Why had they seen so little of him lately? Not that Cecily cared, she told herself. He was a bother and she didn't miss his attentions in the least. But what had he been doing that was so important it had kept him away for two solid weeks? Lord Spenser had seen Cecily several times, but had wisely refrained from mentioning his duel with George, so Cecily remained ignorant and puzzled . . . and very irritated. "I am sick to death of balls," she said crossly as they drove home that night.

"It all does become a terrible bore after a while," said Adriana, eyeing her charge out of the corner of her eye. "And this affair was sadly flat. I do believe our life is falling into a very dull routine." She turned to Cecily. "We have been so busy of late with social obligations we have barely had time to do any shopping. What do you say to devoting ourselves to the simple pleasure of purchasing some new clothes tomorrow?"

Cecily brightened at the suggestion. Some new outfits would surely bring any straying suitors back to heel. "Oh, yes, let's!" she exclaimed.

The next day the ladies set out to take Leicester Square by storm. They visited haberdashers, dressmakers, milliners and corsetieres, and as the morning wore on the number of packages in their landau began to swell to such proportions that they threatened to take over the carriage.

Cecily had acquired a stunning satin fillet, a Norwich shawl and some lilac-colored gloves to go with her new lilac-colored walking dress. Naturally, as shopping required a great deal of energy, the ladies soon found themselves in need of refreshment. After visiting a mantua maker in Mayfair they agreed to visit Gunter's and treat themselves to some delights from that famous confectioner's tea shop.

The establishment was buzzing with people by the time the ladies got there. "We will never find a table," moaned Cecily in disappointment.

"Oh, wait!" cried Adriana. "There is George. I think there is room at his table."

Cecily put on her best smile and looked in the direction her cousin-in-law was heading. The smile turned down at the sight of who George was with. Kate and Albert also shared his table. In her irritation Cecily failed to notice that it was Albert Kate sat next to. She followed her cousin at a slower pace, her irritation taking away her appetite.

Albert had seen their approach. By the time Cecily got to the table they had made room for the newcomers and Adriana was already settling into a chair and visiting with Kate, who gave Cecily a cheery wave. Cecily returned it with a sour smile and unenthusiastically ordered a lemon ice.

"We had thought we might see you last night at Lady Barclay's," Adriana was saying.

George opened his mouth to speak, but before he could say anything Kate spoke up. "Oh, Mr. Atherby joined us in our box at King's Theatre last night, didn't you?"

Albert's mouth dropped open and he looked at Kate as if she'd lost her mind. A swift kick in the shins shut it.

Cecily tossed her head. "Well, we had a very nice time ourselves," she said.

"Mama and Papa just dote on Mr. Atherby," Kate continued. "Why, only this morning Papa said he couldn't remember when he had met a man he liked better." Albert opened his mouth to protest and Kate stuffed a biscuit in it.

Cecily saw none of this. She was glaring at her lemon ice, an angry flush spreading across her cheeks.

"Why, what a nice thing for your papa to say," said Adriana. "Of course, we always knew George was wonderful, did we not, Cecily?"

"Oh, yes," replied Cecily with brittle gaiety. "I am sure we are all glad you are both so happy." Cecily's eyes suddenly felt very watery. She blinked hard. "If you will excuse me I have a sudden headache," she said. She sprang up from her chair, in her haste knocking her lemon ice from the table. It rolled and landed in George's lap with a plop. Cecily turned to Adriana. "May we please go home?"

Adriana was busily exclaiming over George, as were his other companions, so had no immediate answer for Cecily.

Cecily had not waited for one, anyway. She rushed from the crowded establishment, causing heads to turn and a wave of murmuring to follow her as she made her way out the door.

George sat looking at the cold lump oozing yellow rivulets across his leg.

"Oh, George," said Adriana, stifling a giggle. "I am sorry."

George scooped up the yellow mound and put it on the table.

"I say," Albert said to Kate. "What was that all about? If Atherby was with us last night I never saw him."

"That was to make Cecily jealous," said Kate. She looked at her friend's retreating figure. "It certainly seems to have worked. Are your clothes ruined?" she asked George.

"No," said George, grabbing a napkin and wiping his breeches. "They will be fine."

"She didn't even apologize," observed Albert in shocked tones.

"You must forgive Cecily," said Adriana. "I do believe she is a woman in love."

"With Atherby? She has a strange way of showing it!" declared Albert.

If George had been paying attention to his cousin he might have been greatly encouraged by her remark, but his mind had been occupied with the task of mopping up the sticky mess from his leg and trying to understand Cecily's odd behavior. "I think I will go home and get cleaned up," he said. He turned to Kate. "Your real love would probably just as soon have your bogus one gone so he can have you to himself, anyway. Here, Cousin, let me escort you to your carriage."

Cecily was already in the landau by the time George and Adriana arrived. She kept her face averted and refused to look at him. He sighed. The road to true love was not a smooth one.

Adriana wisely said nothing as their carriage threaded its way through the crowded London streets. Finally Cecily's guilty conscience made her speak. "I know I should have apologized to George," she said. "I did not mean to spill my ice in his lap. Really. And I would have said I was sorry, only I was so vexed I could not trust myself to speak. I am sorry to have to say it, Adriana, but your cousin is a shocking flirt."

This was almost too much for Adriana. She pursed her lips in an attempt to stop the betraying smile that tugged at them. Cecily calling George a flirt was very much a case of the pot calling the kettle black.

"A shocking flirt?" echoed her husband later that night. "Is there a side to your cousin which I do not know?"

Adriana giggled. "If there is I am unaware of it. I do believe our Cecily's eyes are changing color. Mayhap she should have bought a green walking dress today. It would have matched her eyes so much better than the lavender one."

"So tell me, love," said Wallingford, settling back against the pillows on his wife's bed, "What is the next act in this farce? Does Cecily now leave off pursuing Spenser and set her cap for George?"

"Why do you ask me? Remember, Gerald. I am no longer involved. I have kept my promise."

"So you have," replied her husband. "But I know you are taking an avid interest in the affair just the same. So give me your opinion. Does it look favorable for our hero?"

Adriana shook her head. "I wonder. She will either make up her mind to have George now that she believes he is behaving so perversely, or she will let irritation drive her into bringing Lord Spenser up to scratch just to punish George. I daresay circumstance will determine what happens next."

"With no help from you," her cynical husband said, sighing.

"Now you are roasting me," Adriana accused and gave

her lord a playful slap on the arm. "There is really nothing more I can do," she said, suddenly serious. "George is on his own."

"A state in which he should have been left all along," observed Wallingford.

His wife pretended not to have heard him.

• 14 •

THE NEXT DAY fate took a hand in the affairs of George and Cecily. Lord Spenser called to solicit the first dance for that evening's ball and to invite Cecily to go driving with him the next week. Lord Spenser's visit, coming as it did after Cecily's last two disastrous meetings with George, gave him a definite edge over his rival. Cecily said yes to both requests.

That night at the ball Cecily saw George leading Lady Penelope onto the floor for a waltz and reminded herself how very glad she was that she was encouraging Lord Spenser in his suit. Really, Cecily fumed, taking in the lady's dampened gown, which clung hungrily to her every curve, if that was the kind of woman whom George Atherby preferred she wished him well. Poor Kate. Did she have any idea what a loose fish Adriana's cousin really was? Cecily thought of warning her friend, and then remembered how unscrupulously Kate had snatched George away from her. A malicious smile played about Cecily's lips. Let the poor dear find out for herself.

George came to Cecily later, asking for a dance. "Every dance is promised," she snapped.

George looked around at the ladies and gentlemen taking their places on the floor for a set of country dances. "It looks as if your partner for this dance has failed to claim you. I shall be happy to let his loss be my gain."

"My feet hurt," said Cecily.

"Already? The evening has barely begun," George protested.

"I do not want to dance with you," said Cecily.

George looked crestfallen, but only for a moment. He sat down in the chair next to hers. "Well, then, if you do not want to dance I shall be glad to keep you company." Cecily did not look glad to have him. George sighed and sat silent, watching the dancers. "Miss Hammond, he said finally, "what have I done to fall into such disfavor?"

Such a straightforward question should have been appreciated by Cecily, but it was not. "I am sure I do not know what you mean," she said, squirming in her chair. But George continued to stare searchingly into her face. "Oh, go away, do!" exclaimed Cecily, exasperated. "Go use that sad puppy look on Lady Penelope. I am sure she would love to see you. In fact, I cannot understand why you are not off fawning over her as you seem to be so smitten. Although I must say I cannot see why you should be taken with someone so old—"

"Lady Penelope!" interrupted George. "Miss Hammond, surely you cannot think I have any interest in Lady Penelope. Why, I only just met the woman at Adriana's."

"You have wasted no time in furthering your acquaintance," Cecily observed tartly. "I saw you dancing with her not more than ten minutes ago."

"It was not I who asked her to dance this evening, but the other way around. Well, almost the other way around. She maneuvered me into asking her to dance."

"Oh, really!" exclaimed Cecily in disgust.

"But it is true. I certainly didn't go looking for her. I was merely standing about watching . . . watching you, if you must know, and wishing I had had the foresight to come by the house earlier and solicit a dance." George's tone turned wistful and his voice trailed off.

Cecily's expression turned soft, and for a moment George hoped she might say something encouraging. But again a look of irritation crossed her face. "It seems you should be explaining yourself to Kate, not me."

"About Kate," George began.

But he was not able to finish. The dance had stopped and Cecily's partner for the next dance came and took her away. George sighed.

Cecily glided across the dance floor as if she didn't have a care in the world. She smiled at her partner and said what any proper young lady should say, but behind her gay façade her mind was racing. What had George been about to say before they were interrupted? It was hard to tell. Oh, and who cared, anyway? She certainly didn't. She was going to bring Lord Spenser up to scratch and become the future Lady Spenser before George Atherby could say Lady Penelope!

When Lord Spenser called to take her driving the next week she gave him her brightest smile as he helped her into his curricle. And as they threaded their way through the streets of Mayfair to Hyde Park she listened raptly while he shared the plans for his latest adventure. "I am racing Farrell to Reigate Wednesday next. It will cost him, poor fellow. He is so sure those showy grays of his will beat my blacks, but it will take more than they have to best mine."

"Your blacks are beautiful," Cecily admitted.

"Beautiful!" Lord Spenser gave an indignant snort. "They are more than that. Prime blood. Sweet goers. There is not a team in London can touch 'em. Except, possibly those chestnuts of your cousin's. And seeing the way he handles the ribbons I'd say he would be a hard man to beat. But Farrell." His lordship chuckled. "I am afraid he will be eating my dust all the way to Reigate. He fancies himself a first-rate whip, another Tommy Onslow. But the poor fellow is hopelessly cowhanded. Only last week he bet Worthington he could turn his curricle round in Sidney's Alley and scraped the paint off the entire right side trying to do so. Of course, I will say this for Farrell. He ain't no crack whip, but he is a regular all-or-nothing boy, so we'll see some sport before the day is over."

Cecily sighed. "It sounds so exciting. How I should like to be in a curricle race."

"Would you?" exclaimed Lord Spenser as they entered the park. "I say, why don't you ride along—to bring me luck. Everything would be all right and proper, for I believe Farrell's sister is accompanying him."

"She is?"

His lordship nodded and chuckled again. "Though why he is bringing her I cannot guess. The girl is anything but a featherweight, and carrying her and his Tiger too is bound to slow him down."

"Oh, but if you took me I would possibly slow you down," said Cecily.

Lord Spenser looked down at her with admiring eyes. "Having you along would add no more weight than a kitten. But it might be dangerous. I suppose your guardian would not allow it and I probably should not have said anything."

Cecily remembered her recent mad adventure with the highwaymen, both real and pretend. If Adriana could engineer such a scheme surely she would have no objection to Cecily going along on a little race. It was, after all, only to Reigate. And since Mr. Farrell's sister was going, she and Lord Spenser would be well chaperoned and everything would be perfectly proper. "How long would it take us to get to Reigate?" she asked.

Lord Spenser considered this. "I can make Reigate easily

in under two hours. Of course, we would have luncheon at the Swan before coming back."

Cecily made some mental calculations. Two hours to Reigate and two hours back plus another hour to eat. Five hours. It was a very long time to be in a gentleman's company. Usually when Lord Spenser took her driving they were only gone for an hour. Well, this was only four hours more. She bit her lip. Perhaps Adriana wouldn't approve. It was rather a long time to be gone.

"We would be making rather a long day of it," said Lord Spenser, echoing her thoughts. But Cecily did not hear him. She had spied a familiar park phaeton only two carriages ahead of them. Kate Courtland sat in it, decked out in an ensemble of lemon yellow. Cecily eyed Kate's bonnet with a critical eye. The silly hat had more plumes than an ostrich, she thought sourly, forgetting she had bought a similar one herself not long ago. Next to Kate rode George, looking like a centaur as he sat the huge horse his cousin had lent him. Kate was directing his attention to something across the park. He made a comment and Kate laughed and shook her head at him.

Cecily's mouth turned down in disgust. Her eyes narrowed and she took a deep breath. She turned to Lord Spenser and, putting on her prettiest smile, said, "I should love to come along and bring you luck. And I know Cousin Gerald and Adriana will have no objection."

"Of course, if they did I would understand perfectly," replied Lord Spenser, with the natural nervousness of a man who was beginning to wonder what he could have been thinking of to invite a female along on a curricle race.

"Oh pooh," said Cecily gaily. "I assure you they shall not care in the least."

"We will have to leave early," said Lord Spenser.

"How early?"

"Well, we are leaving from the Surrey side of Westminster at nine. So I would have to come for you at half past eight."

Again Cecily made some mental calculations. She would have to be up at seven in order to be ready on time. She shuddered inwardly but bravely asserted that she could easily be ready at eight-thirty.

"I must say, Miss Hammond," said Lord Spenser. "Most young ladies would be much too timid to take part in a curricle race."

"Well, I am not at all afraid," asserted Cecily. Then she added coyly, "Besides, with you handling the ribbons I know I shall be perfectly safe."

Lord Spenser preened himself at this bit of flattery and gave his former rival the slightest of nods as they passed George and Kate. Cecily barely acknowledged her former best friend.

"Oh, dear." Kate sighed after they had passed. "I fear she is very angry with me."

"But why?" asked George.

Kate turned wide eyes on him. "You are roasting me, surely. Even after what happened at Gunter's you truly do not know?"

George shook his head, perplexed, and looked even more puzzled as Kate began to laugh. "Oh, you poor, dear man. If I was not already besotted with Albert I vow I would keep you for myself."

George blushed and smiled. "But what has happened between you and Miss Hammond that has made her upset with you?" he asked.

"Why, *you* are what has happened," replied Kate.

George looked even more puzzled and so upset by this that she shook her head at him and smiled. "Cecily is upset because she thinks I have stolen you from her. She is, in a word, jealous."

George's mouth dropped. "Now it is you who is roasting me, Miss Courtland."

"No. I assure you I am not. I believe Cecily thinks more of you that she cares to admit and you have obviously played your part as my admirer so well that she is convinced you have formed an attachment for me. You are indeed a very skilled actor, Mr. Atherby."

Too skilled, perhaps, he thought. "So that is why she has been behaving so strangely toward me," he said thoughtfully.

Kate nodded. "She has finally realized what a prize you are, sir."

A prize, thought George. Me, a prize?

Kate was right. Without his even knowing it, George had begun to blossom once out from under Cecily's nerve-racking stare. It would have been impossible in such a short space of time for George to put on the necessary amount of weight to turn him into a perfect physical specimen. Only the maturity which comes with time and the passage from youth to manhood could do that. But while his physical development was still frustratingly slow, his social skills were developing phenomenally fast. In Miss Courtland's nonthreatening presence George had been able to relax. Her gentle smiles and encouraging flatteries had been enough to give George the confidence he needed, and he now had an air about him that proclaimed him to be a true Regency buck.

George Atherby had acquired something even more important than a massive chest—panache. When the honorable Albert Eagan had taken him under his wing George had found his feet among the ton's young bachelor set. And now that Miss Courtland had taken him in hand he was fast becoming a favorite among the ladies, and the darling of every hostess in London. Mr. Atherby was no duke, nor was he an adonis. But neither was Mr. Atherby high in the instep. A hostess could count on him to dance with the plainest of girls with the greatest of pleasure. And while he seemed to have developed an interest in the lovely Miss Courtland, that never prevented him from complimenting a nervous young lady on her gown or fetching her a cup of punch (which he managed to put in the lady's hand, not on her gown).

If Miss Courtland was correct in her observations, then George had acquired more than panache—he had acquired the interest of the one woman he wanted more than anything in the world. George left Hyde Park and Miss Courtland that day feeling full of hope and optimism. Lady Raine was truly brilliant, it was a wonderful world, and he, George Atherby, was a much better actor than he had ever imagined himself to be.

The next day when he went to Miss Courtland's house to pay a morning call he learned just how very convincing an actor he was. The butler, doing some convincing acting himself, pretended to be deaf to the raised voices coming from the direction of the downstairs drawing room as he took George's hat and gloves and walking stick. He then ushered George into that same room which, with his knock and the announcement of Mr. Atherby's arrival, had become deathly quiet. George gulped uncomfortably at the sight before him. Albert, scowling and red faced, was standing in the middle of the room. At the sight of George his hands clenched into fists. Kate was seated on the sofa. She, too, looked anything but happy to see him. "I am sorry," he said. "I should, perhaps, call at some other time."

"Oh, no, stay," growled Albert. "We were just talking about you."

George's heartbeat quickened, but he bravely forced himself to enter the room and bow over Kate's hand.

"I am afraid Albert is rather put out. You see, Cecily is not the only person we have managed to make jealous."

George's eyes popped out and his mouth dropped open. "No!" he exclaimed.

Kate nodded unhappily.

"I am not jealous," declared Albert. "I am only wondering if the affections of the woman to whom I offered my heart and life—and title—are really engaged to me or not."

This eloquent and impassioned speech seemed so out of character for his friend that George could only collapse into the nearest chair and stare at him.

Kate began to cry. "What a hateful, horrid thing to say. How could you think me so base, so fickle. I only did this to help your friend and see how you turn on me." She retreated into her handkerchief, and George pulled at his cravet, wishing he was elsewhere.

On seeing his beloved burst into tears Albert looked stricken and rushed to kneel by her side. "I am a brute. Please, Kate, forgive me. Here now, please stop crying. Please!"

After what seemed to George an eternity, Kate's sobs turned to sniffles. At last she gave one final sniff and dabbed at her eyes. "Oh, I look a wreck," she moaned.

"You look beautiful," declared Albert worshipfully. "But really, Kate, I don't think I can stand much more of this. How much longer do you two need, anyway?"

Kate looked at George, who squirmed uncomfortably in his chair. "I should say just one more week will do the trick," she said.

"Perhaps we should end this now," George offered. "Cecily already appears to be angry with me. If we make her any more jealous she may not be speaking to me by the end of another week."

"I should hate to quit too early and have all our efforts be for naught," said Kate. "Wouldn't you?"

George looked at Albert, who looked very much as if he wouldn't mind that at all. "Well," he said.

"Only till next week," Kate urged. "I promise you there is nothing between myself and Mr. Atherby but friendship," she said to Albert. "There is only one man I love."

Albert and George both blushed. "Oh, very well," muttered Albert. "But do not play your part so well," he cautioned George. "You will never know how close I came this morning to planting you a facer . . . and then calling you out!"

• 15 •

CECILY DECIDED MERELY to tell her cousin she was going for a morning drive with Lord Spenser, his friend Mr. Farrell, and Mr. Farrell's sister. Even though she knew Adriana was not above staging robberies with phony highwaymen, Cecily wasn't sure she would approve of young ladies taking part in curricle races. Cecily suspected her cousin-in-law might suddenly and inconveniently remember her responsibilities as a guardian and forbid her to accompany Lord Spenser.

And Cecily wanted very much to go. Oh, there would be those stuffy old fusspots who might consider such behavior fast, but surely everything was all perfectly proper since Mr. Farrell and his sister were involved. With two other people along what harm could there be in a little race to Reigate?

Now the question came, when and how should Cecily tell Adriana of her drive? It had to be at a time when Adriana would be preoccupied enough not to ask too many questions, such as when they were leaving, where they were going, and when they would return.

The perfect moment presented itself the next week on the day before the proposed race, when Cecily found Adriana going over the household accounts. Adriana shook her head over a chandler's bill. "The cost of candles is becoming absolutely ridiculous," she muttered. "Twelve shillings a dozen."

"Tomorrow looks to be another fine day," commented Cecily, peering over her cousin-in-law's shoulder.

"Ummmm," agreed Adriana, scribbling busily.

"Lord Spenser is taking me for an early morning drive tomorrow. I hope you did not have plans."

"What's that, dearest? Oh, plans? No, no. That will be fine. Now, why did I order so much ratty powder?" Cecily began to make her escape. "When will you be returning?" asked Adriana.

"I suppose we shall be back early in the afternoon," Cecily replied vaguely, her hand on the door handle.

"Early? That is fine. I am sure you will have a splendid time," Adriana said generously, giving Cecily a distracted smile.

"I shall," said Cecily. "Thank you." Then she slipped out the door before Adriana could question her more closely, feeling pleased that she had secured her guardian's permission for her outing—a fact of which she could remind Adriana the next day if she became upset by Cecily's late return.

Cecily went back to her room and began to plan what she would wear for her big adventure. What she needed to complete her ensemble and properly impress Lord Spenser, Cecily finally concluded, was a new bonnet. She decided to risk another visit to Adriana.

Adriana still sat staring at her pile of household bills. "Adriana, would you mind terribly if I were to go shopping this morning?" asked Cecily.

Adriana looked up from her work, a look of irritation flitting across her face. "What did you say?"

"I said I should like to go shopping."

"Oh, Cecily. I am buried up to my nose in accounts that

simply have to be gone over this morning," replied Adriana.

"I didn't mean you had to come with me. I will take Sarah."

"Oh, very well," said Adriana distractedly. "Have a good time."

"I shall," said Cecily gaily and she skipped from the room. Of course she would have a good time. There was nothing more entertaining than finding lovely clothes with which to make one's self even more beautiful. And Cecily intended to look very beautiful the next day. Lord Spenser would be properly impressed with what he saw when he came to fetch her. Between her striking good looks and her adventurous spirit she knew he would be unable to resist offering for her before the day was over.

With her maid for protection, Cecily set off in the direction of Oxford Street, where she had seen just the hat for her outing in a shop window.

Once within sight of Oxford Street Cecily decided to leave the carriage and walk so she could browse in some other shops before visiting the milliners. She instructed Samson, the coachman, and the footman to wait, and, with Sarah firmly in tow, set off in search of fashion treasure. It was still fairly early in the morning for most of the ton, and the streets were pleasantly uncrowded. How very nice, thought Cecily as she made her way down the flagway, not to be so jostled.

She stopped and looked longingly at the exotic wares displayed in the window of W.H. Botibol, plummassier. A gypsy hat would hardly do for a curricle race, but it would be perfect for Lady Ethelrod's alfresco party, which was coming up the next week. Cecily's pin money was running low, but surely she could afford a few ostrich plumes. Some plumes dyed pink would look so lovely with her pink muslin gown. And possibly the milliner would give her a bargain on a wide-brimmed hat if she purchased that charming bonnet.

Cecily ogled the plumes with a greedy eye, in much the same manner the two gentlemen across the street were watching her. Sarah caught sight of them and tugged on her mistress' sleeve. "Look, miss," she whispered.

Cecily followed Sarah's nervous gaze and saw the two Bond Street beaus lounging across the street. One of them tipped his hat and the other let out a low whistle. Cecily blushed and tossed her curls. "Come along, Sarah," she ordered, and marched off down the flagway.

The two men crossed the street and sauntered along after them, and Cecily could feel her heart begin to pound. She ducked into a corsetiere's and for the next ten minutes pretended an interest in ladies unmentionables which she was far from feeling. "That should have given them plenty of time to move on," she said to Sarah as they opened the door. "Now we will just step down the street a few doors and I will purchase that bonnet, and then we may go home." She turned to walk down the flagway and gave a startled cry. There in the next doorway lounged the same two men. Surely they couldn't do anything to her in a public street, Cecily reasoned. And with her maid right there with her! But the ungentlemanly looks they were giving her made her nervous all the same. With a bravery she was far from feeling she marched up to them and said, "If you gentlemen do not stop following me and staring so rudely I shall hit you with my parasol."

"Oh," said the taller one to his companion. "We have a regular tigress here. Are you out by yourself, miss, with only a maid to escort you?"

"My carriage is right down the street," said Cecily in

threatening tones. "And I have but to call and my driver will be here instantly."

"But what if your driver has fallen asleep? Perhaps my friend and I should escort you . . ."

Cecily marched off before the man could finish. She heard a low chuckle and the sound of her tormentors' footsteps behind her. Or was that her heart pounding in her ears? She stepped up her pace and bit her lip to keep from crying.

"Miss Hammond," called a voice. "I say, Miss Hammond!"

Cecily turned around to see George running across the street in her direction, coattails flapping. The two men had also seen him and turned and strolled away. Cecily sighed a shakey sigh. "Oh, how glad I am to see you!" she exclaimed. "Those two men were following me and being most rude."

George nodded. "I thought so," he said. "A woman out with only her maid this early in the day is not always safe from ungentlemanly behavior. Where are you bound? Would you like me to escort you?"

"Oh, yes," said Cecily eagerly, forgetting that only a few days ago she had been very angry with George Atherby, that shocking flirt. She put a tiny gloved hand through his arm and looked at him as if he had saved her from being ravished instead of merely harassed. "I was just going to buy a new bonnet."

They walked companionably to the milliner's shop and George gave his opinion on the various creations Cecily placed on her head. He managed to further ingratiate himself with his love by admiring the very hat she liked best. "I must say," she told him as they left the milliners, "I never realized what excellent taste you had in clothes."

"Oh, I don't know that my taste is so very remarkable,"

replied George. "I think you would look beautiful in almost anything."

Cecily regarded him from under her lashes. "Do you?" she asked.

"I think you are incomparably beautiful," said George.

"Incomparably?" repeated Cecily dubiously.

"Why, yes."

"I rather thought you preferred a lighter coloring. And reddish-colored hair," ventured Cecily.

This has gone far enough, thought George. "There is something I should like to tell you about Kate," he began.

Cecily stiffened.

"It all started after . . ."

Someone yelling a hallo from down the street interrupted him. Cecily scowled and George looked to see Kate and Albert strolling in their direction. George swore under his breath. "Here," he said suddenly. "Would you not like to look in this shop?"

Cecily objected strongly as George tried to steer her through the door and into the corsetiere's where she had taken refuge only an hour before. "I should say not!" she exclaimed, her cheeks flaming. "Anyway, it is too late for you to hide, for Kate has seen us. My carriage is just up ahead. I believe I can safely make it on my own now. Thank you for your assistance, sir, and good day." Cecily marched off with Sarah close behind.

George hesitated. Should he chase after Cecily and try to explain? Cecily thought he had tried to dodge Kate because of a guilty conscience. In reality he had only wanted to dodge her before she could help him anymore and further tangle what he felt was fast becoming a very disadvantageous misunderstanding between Cecily and himself. Best catch her, he told himself. "Miss Hammond," he called, as Cecily got into her carriage. George ran down the flagway in an attempt to overtake her and collided with a ladies' maid, sending himself and her mistress' packages sprawling. Cecily's carriage drove off without any further protest from George. He was too busy picking up parcels and apologizing to the irate dowager lecturing him.

"Atherby!" exclaimed Alfred, tearing his friend away from the red-faced woman. "What was that all about?"

"Cecily," replied George sadly.

"That woman was giving you a bear garden jaw over Cecily?" Albert exclaimed in disbelief.

"What? Oh, no," said George. "I was chasing Cecily. I was trying to explain to her about Kate and myself. But I never caught her because I ran into that woman's maid."

"Oh, poor Mr. Atherby," said Kate, patting George's shoulder. "You must not worry so. It will all work out. You'll see." She slipped her hand through his arm and led him off down the street. Albert followed behind wearing a pout.

"We were having such a wonderful time," mused George. "I was going to ask her to go driving with me."

"Would you like me to speak to Cecily, and explain?" Kate offered.

George shook his head. "Thank you, but no. I should talk to her myself."

"All right," said Kate. "But let us put our heads together before you do and see if we can discover the best way to go about straightening things out. I am sure she loves you."

"It is getting curst hard to tell who loves who anymore," grumbled Albert, but neither of his companions paid any attention to him.

George was not the only one feeling unhappy with the day's turn of events. Cecily looked unseeing out the carriage window and drummed her fingers angrily on her reticule. Once again the provoking George Atherby had set her to fuming. The beast! How dare he rescue her from those horrid men and make her think he wanted to spend his morning with her when all along he had been shopping with Kate. Who did he think he was, anyway? And did he think that she, Cecily Hammond, the toast of the season, need waste her time with the likes of him? Why, she could have her pick of any number of men more suitable than George Atherby. Lord Evanston adored the ground she walked on. Hadn't he said so only last week? Sir Winston would most likely offer for her before the season was out. And Lord Spenser would offer for her before the day was out tomorrow. She would make sure of that. And she would accept him, too! George Atherby, that shocking flirt, would be sorry. And Kate would be sorry, too. She would discover what a cad George was and be very sorry, indeed. They'd all be sorry! Angry tears stung Cecily's eyes and she blinked them back. With a toss of her head she alighted from her carriage and swept into the house as if she had not a care in the world. Soon she would be the future Lady Spenser. And when that happened she would make sure that George Atherby was the first to hear of it.

The next morning Cecily's maid dutifully woke her at seven. It was an effort to stir from her bed, although a fire was lit and burning gaily, its warmth already spreading out to take the early morning chill from the bedroom. Cecily had slept fitfully during the wee morning hours, waking every hour, waiting for seven o'clock to come and bring the beginning of her great adventure. As is often the case when sleep has been slow in coming, waking was hard and the thought of staying in bed was an inviting one. But excitement won over and she forced herself to set her feet on the cold floor and scamper to the thick rug in front of the fire, letting it warm her before her maid helped her from her nightgown and into her clothes.

By twenty after eight Cecily stood outside the front door dressed in a merino pelisse with three capes and a silk scarf, blue kid slippers, and a bonnet with as many plumes as the one she had scorned on her friend only a few days earlier. At the sight of his lordship's curricle she ran down the steps and out to the gate.

"You are ready on time!" Lord Spenser exclaimed in surprise as he jumped down to help her up.

"I should not want to keep you waiting on such an important day," Cecily said.

"Never even heard of a female who could be ready on time for anything, much less known one," remarked Lord Spenser. "You are truly remarkable, Miss Hammond. Well," he said, climbing up beside her, "adventure calls. Right, Daniel?" he flung over his shoulder.

"Yessir," his tiger answered, giving Cecily a gap-toothed grin.

Lord Spenser cracked his whip and his restless horses broke into a brisk trot. Cecily smiled to herself. This was even more exciting than a masked ball. And somehow she knew she would never forget this day.

They reached the starting point only a few minutes ahead of their competition. Cecily knew the honorable Frederick Farrell, although not well. He was not one of the circle of her devoted admirers, mainly because, as he put it, he was not much in the petticoat line. The honorable Mr. Farrell's one burning desire was to become a member of the elite Four-in-Hand club. But his skill, or rather lack of it, barred him from membership.

As his curricle came careening into view Cecily could see why the members of this fraternity preferred to make their dashing pilgrimage to Salt Hill without him. Farrell's horses appeared out of control and his curricle was already swaying dangerously. His sister, a plump young woman with plain features and mousy brown hair, was clinging tightly to the side with one hand and holding her bonnet with the other. Her face was a study in terror, her eyes wide and her mouth open as if in a silent scream.

Lord Spenser grinned and shook his head. "If Farrell's sister don't expire from palpitations before the day is over I will be surprised. Ho there, Farrell," he called. "Good morning, Miss Farrell."

Miss Farrell let out a sigh of relief as her brother slowed his horses to a walk and pulled up next to them. She greeted Cecily cordially and wished Lord Spenser good fortune.

"He will need it," Farrell said, laughing, "I am in fine form today."

"So we see," said Lord Spenser. "Well, then, turn your rig around and let's be gone."

"Right-o," said Farrell, pulling back on the reins and trying to turn his horses around at the same time. Cecily watched the wheel of his curricle brush dangerously near theirs and bit her lip.

"I say, Farrell," called Lord Spenser over the clatter of hooves. "Wouldn't it be easier to drive straight on and turn round? Then you could come up beside us."

"By Jove, you've got a point there," agreed Farrell, cracking his whip.

Cecily turned and watched, fascinated by Mr. Farrell's progress. The driver of a passing carriage swore at him as he nearly collided with it while turning his curricle. Finally, assisted by a series of squeaks and wild gesticulations from his sister, the honorable Frederick Farrell managed to get his curricle headed in the right direction and pulled up alongside his competitor.

"Are we ready, then?" called Lord Spenser.

"Ready," Farrell called back.

"Then we're off." Lord Spenser turned to Cecily. "Give us the signal to go, Miss Hammond."

Cecily was delighted with the privilege granted her and called out, "To the ready—Go!"

The gentlemen cracked their whips and the horses sprang forward. Lord Spenser's curricle took off with a great jerk, throwing Cecily back against the seat. She laughed in excitement and waved at Miss Farrell. Miss Farell's attention, however, was fully occupied in hanging on to her seat. Cecily couldn't help wondering why the poor girl had agreed to come along on this race. She obviously didn't have the disposition for it, Cecily concluded, feeling very superior.

Farrell's curricle began to pull ahead of them and Cecily watched in consternation as the gap widened. "Oh, they are getting ahead of us!" she cried.

"For the moment. But at the rate he is springing 'em we will pass him on the first hill."

Lord Spenser was right. They soon gained on their competitors and passed them. Cecily laughed and waved gaily as they raced by. Soon the distance between the two curricles was so great the other couple and their horses looked like small toys to Cecily. They went down a hill and the Farrells were completely lost from sight. "Oh, splendid!" cried Cecily. "They shall never catch us now, will they?"

"I doubt it," said Lord Spenser. "But we will keep up this pace a little longer just to be sure."

Cecily looked once more over her shoulder and smiled with glee. This was great fun and she wouldn't have missed it for the world.

Lord Spenser finally felt free to slow his horses a bit and they went through Croyden at a leisurely pace. They had seen no sign of the Farrells for the last five miles and Cecily would have liked to take a few minutes to stretch her legs and freshen up. Lord Spenser, however, made no mention of stopping so she kept her wishes to herself.

When they came to Merstham, however, she suggested a quick stop. "Just for a few minutes," she assured Lord Spenser. "I am sure we have time. I have not seen even a glimpse of them this last hour or more."

Lord Spenser pulled his watch from his waistcoat. "Let's push on to Reigate. It is almost time for nuncheon and the Swan has the best food of any inn on the Brighton road."

There were many reasons why Cecily was feeling the need to stop, and the one uppermost in her mind was not one a lady could mention to a gentleman. "We *must* stop. I simply cannot go any further until I have had a few moments to stretch," she said firmly.

"Oh, very well," Lord Spenser replied grudgingly. "Here," he said, indicating an inn up ahead. "We shall have something to drink and take a moment for a quick stretch."

They pulled up in front of the fine-looking timbered edifice. Many of the coaches bound for Brighton stopped in Merstham, so its innkeeper was used to catering to travelers in a hurry. Lord Spenser jumped down and stretched his legs while his tiger walked the horses and made sure they got something to drink. Cecily disappeared in search of that facility most important to travelers. She barely had time to drink the fresh cider the landlord pressed upon her before Lord Spenser hurried her back into the curricle. With another crack of the whip and another jerk of the curricle they were off again, Cecily holding onto her bonnet.

Lord Spenser drove his horses hard the last few miles to Reigate and it seemed to Cecily that the trees and fields fairly flew by. His lordship took out his watch as they pulled up in front of the Swan. "Just under two hours!" he declared. "That must be a new record." He jumped down from the curricle and ran around to help Cecily down. "At that rate poor old Farrell couldn't have caught us even if he could drive. There's no finer pair in England," he concluded, patting a foam-specked rump as his tiger led the team away. "Would you like to see something of the town before we eat?" he asked politely.

"Yes, I should," replied Cecily, wishing she could rub her sore bottom. "I do feel a little cramped."

Lord Spenser chuckled. "You're a right one, Miss Hammond. Pluck to the backbone."

• 16 •

ADRIANA WAS MOMENTARILY puzzled when Cecily didn't come down for breakfast. Then she recalled her charge mentioning something about a drive with Lord Spenser. Was that today? But surely she wouldn't have gone out before breakfast! Adriana sent for the little maid she had hired to attend Cecily. "Sarah, was Miss Cecily to go driving with Lord Spenser today?"

Sarah's eyes grew wide and she gulped. "Yes, ma'am," she whispered.

"Has she set out already, then?" asked Adriana.

"Yes, ma'am," replied Sarah. "She said to tell you that Mr. Farrell and his sister were going with them and that she wouldn't be back until afternoon, so not to feel you must wait for her return if you had something you needed to do today."

This speech was delivered in a rush. Her mission accomplished, Sarah stood in such obvious terror and desire to be gone that Adriana could not help but smile. "Goodness, child. I am not such an ogre that I will bite your head off merely because my cousin won't be back till after nuncheon. We are not her gaolers."

"No, ma'am," Sarah said and bit her lip.

"Thank you, Sarah, you may go," said Adriana, dismissing the maid with a wave of her hand. She shook her head and smiled as the girl made good her escape. The child was afraid of her own shadow!

Adriana went through her morning's duties in a cheerful ignorance of Cecily's activities. She did stop once to wonder why Cecily had not mentioned that she and Lord Spenser would be meeting other people. And what were they doing that was going to keep her gone until afternoon? Were they properly chaperoned? A frown creased Adriana's forehead as she tried to remember just what Cecily had said to her the morning before. Was Cecily up to something? Adriana shook her head. Her cousin was a strong-minded young lady, but Adriana didn't think her charge had the imagination to scheme her way into mischief. Still, it was all very odd. However, there was little sense in worrying about something over which she had no control, thought Adriana. Yet her mind seemed determined to fret. In search of distraction she paid a morning call on her sister-in-law.

"But where is Cecily?" asked Elizabeth as the tea things were brought in.

"Driving with Lord Spenser," said Adriana, helping herself to a biscuit.

"Again? It does begin to look as though she will bring him up to scratch."

"Yes, I think so. But I think she is beginning to realize that it is not really Lord Spenser she wants," said Adriana.

"Never tell me our plan is working."

Adriana nodded and took the proferred teacup. "I believe it is." She sighed. "I do begin to wonder if Gerald was not right after all and we shouldn't have interferred."

"Nonsense," said Elizabeth stoutly. She eyed her sister-in-law. "That is not all that is bothering you, is it?"

"No," admitted Adriana. "I fear I am allowing Cecily too much freedom."

"Too much freedom? You are almost never apart."

Adriana took a meditative sip of tea. "Do you know she went driving with Lord Spenser this morning and left me a message not to expect her back until afternoon?"

"Afternoon?" echoed Elizabeth.

Adriana nodded. "And not only Lord Spenser, but his friend Mr. Farrell and his sister were to be of the party. And she never said anything about that when she mentioned her drive the other day."

"Well," said Elizabeth, "at least they are not alone."

"I hardly think the honorable Mr. Farrell and his sister qualify as chaperons," said Adriana. "If I didn't know better I would swear she was up to something."

Elizabeth laughed. "You must not judge everyone by the workings of your own devious mind, dearest. But I must admit this is making herself a little too free. You will most likely have to talk to her when she returns."

"Yes," agreed Adriana. "And I do not relish it. I feel I have lost Cecily's respect ever since our farce on Hounslow Heath."

"That was unfortunate," agreed Elizabeth. "But come now, you are refining too much upon this. A shopping expedition will do much to raise your spirits. I was going to go out. Why not accompany me? We shall enjoy an orgy of spending and you will feel much better."

Adriana smiled and shook her head. "No. I think I shall scoot back home and wait for Cecily to reappear."

So Adriana returned home and Elizabeth ventured out to entertain herself among the fashionable shops in the new Regent Street. One bonnet and two pairs of gloves later she decided to treat her palate with a visit to Gunter's. It was close to teatime and the shop was filling with ladies and gentlemen who had a similar mission in mind.

At a table by the window Elizabeth caught sight of a familiar face. George waved and beckoned her to the table where he was sitting with Miss Courtland and a slightly chunky young man with reddish brown hair and a snub nose. Elizabeth blinked at the sight of George's companion. "How very curious," she muttered.

Meanwhile, George was pulling a chair from the neighboring table up next to Miss Courtland. "Only fancy meeting you here," he said cheerfully as Elizabeth sat down. "Miss Courtland has been helping me shop for a fan for Cecily. Would you care to see it?"

"Yes, George. It is nice to see you, too," replied Elizabeth distractedly. "But Mr. Farrell, what are you doing here? Were you not supposed to be somewhere with Miss Hammond and Lord Spenser today?"

"Reigate," said the honorable Frederick Farrell sadly. "I was supposed to be at Reigate."

"Reigate!" exclaimed his companions in unison.

Farrell took out his watch and examined it. He sighed. "Yes. They're probably on their way back by now."

"But why Reigate—and why are you not with them?" asked Elizabeth, her voice rising. A look from Miss Courtland reminded her of her surroundings and she bit her lip.

"We were to race to Reigate. Bet my team (and a good deal of blunt) against his that I could beat Spenser. I would have, too, except my sister took sick. The girl has the weakest constitution. Don't know why I ever let her come along. We were barely out of town when she . . ." Farrell shuddered. "All over the upholstery," he confided in a whisper to George. "There was nothing for it but to take her home. She was hysterical. Of course, when my mother heard about it . . ." He shook his head. "It was terrible. I finally escaped and decided to go for a toddle around town. Ran into Atherby here, and Miss Courtland. Invited me along and here we are. And that is why I am not in Reigate."

The others at the table exchanged uneasy glances.

"Then Cecily and Lord Spenser do not know you returned to town," ventured Miss Courtland.

Farrell thought on this a moment. "By jove, they don't!" he exclaimed. "You don't suppose they are still waiting for me at the Swan, do you?"

"As they have no idea what has become of you they are most likely either waiting still, or fearing you have met with a mishap and are scouring the surrounding countryside for you," Elizabeth informed him.

George looked at Elizabeth. "They are unchaperoned. And if they are still at the Swan they will never make it back before dark."

Farrell let out a low whistle. "You know, I never thought of that. The experience with my sister had me so upset—and then with my mother ripping up at me, well, it just pushed all thought of Spenser right out of my mind."

Miss Courtland looked at him in disgust, then turned to Elizabeth. "What's to do?" she asked.

George was already on his feet. "I shall rent a gig and go look for them."

"Wait. I will come with you," said Kate, gathering her reticule and parasol. "Mama will probably not be back from Lady Snelling's yet, but I shall leave her a note so she won't worry."

George was anxious to be gone as quickly as possible. "Perhaps I should go alone," he suggested tactfully.

"I want to help," said Kate. She laid an imploring hand on his arm. "Cecily is my friend. Please let me come with you. I may not be of any use, but I will feel so much better if you allow me to come along. I promise I shan't hold you up long."

George nodded and smiled at her. "Very well," he said.

"Charles and I shall follow as soon as I have gotten word to Adriana," said Elizabeth, also rising.

"Oh, dear," said Kate. "Albert was coming to dinner tonight. Mr. Farrell, perhaps you would be so good as to stop at his lodgings on your way home and tell him where we are bound. We may need his help."

The cause of all the trouble was also now on his feet, looking very penitent and only too happy to be of service. He would have been happy to come along and help them look for Miss Hammond and Lord Spenser, he explained, but his mama had ordered him to return that night and escort her and his sister to Almack's. And if he didn't show up after what happened earlier, "Well, you know what females are," he said to George. "Anyhow, I am sure you can have no trouble finding them. We were going by way of Croyden, then Merstham, and you are bound to meet up with them at one of those towns."

George merely glowered at Farrell before offering Miss Courtland his arm and escorting her from the crowded establishment. Elizabeth and the chagrined-looking Farrell followed behind.

The honorable Mr. Frederick Farrell was indeed a young man of honor, if nothing else, and so, feeling truly repentant for his act of selfish forgetfulness, he decided to try and find Albert and deliver Miss Courtland's message in person. Who knew how long it would be before Eagan got the message if he left it at his lodgings, Farrell reasoned, so he headed off in search of Albert. His first stop was Jackson's boxing salon. When he got there he learned he had missed the honorable Mr. Eagan by less than an hour. Someone said they thought Eagan bound for Tattersall's, so Frederick followed him there only to learn he had again missed his quarry, this time by a mere ten minutes. Since he was there he paused to inspect some prime cattle which he liked even better than the grays he had that day forfeited to Lord Spenser. And before he left he was the proud owner of the nicest pair of chestnuts he had ever laid eyes on and feeling, in spite of all the small misfortunes which had befallen him, a very lucky man.

Of course, he had still not located Albert, and no one at Tattersall's had any idea where his next destination was. As Farrell had already spent two hours looking for him, he judged that in the interest of time he had best go to Albert's lodgings and leave a message after all. Having finally accomplished this, Farrell went on his way secure in the knowledge that he had now discharged all his social obligations, and he dismissed all thought of the fate of Miss Hammond and Lord Spenser from his mind.

Albert returned to his lodgings only ten minutes after Farrell had left his message—an unfortunate thing, since the message was a little vague. Albert's eyes widened in astonished anger as he read: "Missed you at Jackson's and Tatt's. Atherby and Miss Courtland are on their way to Reigate. Suggest you follow as soon as you can. Your obedient, Farrell."

"Follow as soon as I can. I should say I will!" growled Albert. He crumpled the note and hurled it at the hearth. Bellowing for his driving cape and gloves, he rushed from the room.

Shortly thereafter he was seen bowling down the street on his way to Westminster Bridge. He was halfway across town when he missed Lord Wallingford's curricle by a bare inch, and wouldn't have stopped had not Wallingford hailed him. Albert ground his teeth and pulled his horses to a stop. "Good day, your lordship," he said coldly.

"Is it? From the look on your face I would guess this day

to be anything but good for you. May I ask what is the matter?"

"Since you ask, sir, I will tell you. Your wife's cousin is the matter," replied Albert curtly. "I have received a message that he and my betrothed have run off together and are bound for Reigate."

"Gretna is the other direction. Surely there must be a logical explanation for this," ventured Wallingford.

"There certainly is," snapped Albert. "Gretna or no Gretna, your cousin-in-law has run off with my intended! Now, if you will excuse me—" Albert cracked his whip and his curricle plunged forward.

Wallingford pushed back his curly brimmed beaver and scratched his head. Coming to a sudden decision, he turned his horses toward home.

Twenty minutes later Wallingford strolled into the drawing room and found his wife pacing the floor. "Oh, it is you," she sighed.

Wallingford cocked an cyebrow at her. "Yes. I am sorry to disappoint you."

Adriana gave him a small smile. "I was hoping you were Cecily."

"Alas, I am not," he said.

"Cecily has gone out with Lord Spenser and not yet returned. She has been gone all day and I am becoming quite worried about her."

"She has been gone all day, you say," said Wallingford, rubbing his chin thoughtfully. "Fetch your bonnet, love," he said suddenly. "We are going for a drive."

"Gerald, you do not understand. I really must wait here until Cecily returns. I was going over the household accounts when she asked my permission to go driving with Lord Spenser, and I am afraid I did not pay very close attention to what she was saying. I never dreamed she would be gone all day. Oh, Gerald, I have no idea where she has gone," Adriana finished on a wail.

"I believe I do," said Wallingford.

Adriana stared at him. "What?"

"Come, love," he said, taking her hand and leading her from the room. "We need to go save your cousin from disaster, and I have a strong feeling we shall find mine while we are doing so." Adriana looked at her lord as if he had lost his mind. He smiled mysteriously at her and said, "I will tell you all about it on the way."

• 17 •

THE HIGH HILL leading to Reigate afforded a very fine view but the town itself held little appeal for Cecily. In her eyes it was old and half ruined. Not even its shops were tempting. And her stomach was beginning to rumble. So she heartily agreed when Lord Spenser suggested they abandon waiting for their rival and seek sustenance.

Their meal at the Swan consisted of a boiled fowl and sauce, oysters, potted charr, tarts and three or four sweetmeats, all washed down by several tankards of ale for the gentleman and some fresh cider for the lady. Needless to say, eating occupied a good hour of their time. There was much to talk over—the skill with which Lord Spenser had handled the ribbons, the excellent time they had made, the sad difference between the shops of Reigate and those of London. But finally conversation began to flag and Lord Spenser took out his watch. "It is after two. He should have been here over two hours ago," he said, shaking his head.

"You don't suppose they have met with some fatal accident," suggested Cecily. "The way Mr. Farrell handles his horses I should not be surprised to find them overturned in a ditch somewhere."

"Oh, Farrell's bad, but he ain't that bad," said Lord Spenser.

"I don't know," said Cecily doubtfully. "Why are they not here? You said yourself they should have arrived over two hours ago. What other possible explanation could there be?"

Lord Spenser rubbed his chin. "You may be right. At any rate we cannot wait any longer for them. We should be starting back. We can look for them along the way."

So they climbed back into his lordship's curricle and began retracing their steps, Cecily scanning the road ahead as well as every side road for any sign of an overturned carriage with two broken bodies laying somewhere near it.

They were a little over a mile outside of Merstham and had still seen no sign of Mr. Farrell and his sister, wounded or otherwise, when a large wagonful of hay lumbered into sight.

As the wagon drew nearer it became increasingly clear to Cecily that the road would not accommodate both it and their curricle. How Lord Spenser would get around it she couldn't begin to guess because at this point a ditch ran along each side of the road. Lord Spenser did not seem to be concerned at all. In fact, to her alarm he urged his horses to pick up speed. "What are you doing?" she demanded. "Do slow down or we will have a mishap."

"Nonsense," replied Lord Spenser confidently. "Now, Miss Hammond, you shall see some truly skillful driving."

Cecily had already seen plenty of derring-do that morning. She had no desire to see any more. She just wanted to reach London in one piece. She looked at the driver of the wagon, a large youth with vacant eyes and a mouth that hung open, and realized he would never figure out unassisted that he was coming straight down the middle of the road and leaving no room for oncoming traffic. There was only one thing to do. Bracing her hand on his lordship's shoulder she stood up and began gesticulating and calling to the boy to move over.

"Here now," said Lord Spenser, his concentration broken. "What are you doing?"

"I am trying to get him to move over," replied Cecily, her voice rising in irritation. "Look at all the room he has on the other side. He is going to crowd us off the road. Move over!" she called again.

"Here now, Miss Hammond," said his lordship, trying to direct his horses and reseat Cecily at the same time. "You must sit down." He grabbed ahold of one of the capes on her pelisse and yanked firmly, toppling Cecily back onto the seat. The curricle rocked and the horses began to prance nervously.

"We are going to tip over," Cecily squeaked. Again she tried to motion the hay wagon aside. It was almost upon them and Lord Spenser's horses took exception to their less thoroughbred cousins which were pulling it and began to dance about in earnest. Cecily was still trying to regain her feet and stop disaster, all the while making the curricle sway dangerously.

The wagon squeezed by just as the right wheel of the curricle went over the edge of the road. Like a ship sinking at sea the carriage slowly tipped and landed on its side, throwing a screeching Cecily onto the bank. She had been frantically clawing at Lord Spenser and, with her fingers firmly entwined in his coat sleeve, she managed to pull him off, too. He landed on top of her in a most compromising position which, in spite of the fact he had been keeping a mistress for almost a year, made him blush.

His embarrassment quickly turned to anger as he climbed off Cecily and surveyed his bright yellow toy laying broken on the side of the road, his tiger trying to calm the frightened horses. "Why on earth did you not sit still as I asked you to?" he growled, clambering down the bank and onto the road.

Cecily stood up to dust herself off but her legs had turned to jelly. She collapsed again on the bank and took a deep breath to calm herself. She glared at Lord Spenser, who was at his horse's heads and talking gently to the animals. "You might at least ask if I am all right," she snapped.

Lord Spenser regarded her coldly. "Are you all right?" he asked.

"Yes, thank you," she said haughtily. "And now that your horses are calmed down and that wagon is out of the way perhaps we may continue."

"Yes, we may continue," said Lord Spenser. "But we shall have to do so without my curricle. The axle is broken and a wheel has come off."

Cecily looked in dismay at the broken curricle. She watched the disappearing cloud of dust and the vanishing wagon, whose simpleminded driver had not paused for more than an amazed look before continuing on his way. "But how shall we get back to London?" she wailed.

"We are only a little over a mile from Merstham. We shall have to walk there and get help."

"Walk!" cried Cecily.

"You may ride one of my horses," his lordship offered.

"I never ride without a sidesaddle," Cecily informed him.

"Well, I am sorry, but I have not got one with me," snapped his lordship.

"Then I shall walk," she said, rising.

"As you wish," he replied. His tiger unhooked the horses from their harness and began to lead them off down the road while Lord Spenser helped Cecily down from the bank.

"What shall we do when we get to Merstham?" she asked as they began walking.

"I shall try and find a wheelwright to repair my curricle."

"But that could take hours," Cecily protested.

"Have you a better idea?" asked Lord Spenser.

"We must hire a post chaise and get back to London immediately."

"I shall do my best," said Lord Spenser, "to get you back to London as quickly as possible. But I must tell you I have not much money with me. I did not anticipate any such thing as this happening."

"Can you not pawn something?" asked Cecily desperately.

Lord Spenser looked pardonably perturbed at this. "Miss Hammond, I shall do everything in my power to get you back home as soon as I may. But, really, I think you are refining upon this too much. After all, your family knows of this and they will surely come looking for us when . . ." Lord Spenser's sentence trailed off as the reason for the guilty look on Cecily's face dawned on him. "Miss Hammond. You did tell your family where we were bound, did you not?"

Cecily nervously twisted her fingers. "Not exactly."

Lord Spenser's lips compressed into a thin line. "If it is not being unreasonable, might I ask what you did tell them?"

Cecily drew herself up with as much dignity as she could muster. "I merely informed my cousin that we were going driving."

"My God!" gasped Lord Spenser.

"I did leave word that Mr. Farrell and his sister would be with us, but they are not," she finished miserably.

"So they have no idea where we are," Lord Spenser said in the voice of a condemned man.

Cecily shook her head. A tear rolled down her cheek.

"If that is the case then Miss Hammond I must beg of you—"

"Do not beg anything of me," interrupted Cecily crossly.

"This is all your fault. If you had only slowed down back there as I asked we would be halfway home by now."

Lord Spenser's eyes narrowed. "Is that so?"

"Yes, it is!" cried Cecily. "Oh, my feet! When will we be there?"

"When we have spent as much energy walking as we have in arguing," snapped her companion, picking up his pace.

Cecily had taken off her slipper to remove a pebble from it. She considered hurling it at Lord Spenser, but thought better of it and put it back on. He had continued to walk, not waiting for her, and she had to run to catch up with him. "You might at least slow down," she said.

"Madam. The sooner we get to town the sooner I can dispatch you to London. And right now there is nothing I would rather do."

Cecily's eyes grew wide. "Well! That is fine with me. I must say," she huffed as they continued down the road, "I have certainly seen a side to your character, sir, which I have never seen before."

"I might say the same thing," replied his lordship.

"And what, pray, does that mean?" asked Cecily, grabbing his arm and stopping him.

Lord Spenser sighed. "I am sorry. Please forgive me," he said, trying to regain his manners.

"No. I want to hear what you were about to say."

Lord Spenser shook his head and commenced walking again.

Cecily didn't move. Her eyes narrowed and her hands flew to her hips. Then Miss Cecily Hammond sat down in the middle of the road.

Lord Spenser, on realizing his companion had not fallen in step with him, turned around and saw her sitting there, arms crossed and a stubborn look on her face. "May I ask what you are doing?" he said through clenched teeth.

"I am not moving until you finish what you started to say. Pray, what have you seen in my character to provoke you so?"

"All right, madam, since you insist on knowing I will tell you. First, by deceiving your family and slipping off for this outing without telling them where you were bound, you have placed us in a very delicate position. I am honor bound to offer for you, which I had intended doing anyway. But," he continued, taking her hand and yanking her to her feet, "I tell you now that I would rather be sued for my entire fortune and thrown in jail than be forced to marry such a sharp-tongued, spoiled female as yourself."

"Sharp-tongued! Spoiled!" spluttered Cecily. "Why, you horrid brute!" For what she did next Cecily must be pardoned. It had been a long day. She was worried that Adriana would be so displeased with her she would send her packing back to her mama before she could achieve a brilliant match. She had had too much excitement and her nerves were well beyond frayed. This was the final straw. She drew back her prettily shod foot and kicked Lord Spenser in the shin with all her might. Feeling much better she left him hopping and swearing in the middle of the road and resumed her hike. At the sound of his footsteps behind her she turned and said, "How the man who wrote me such a beautiful poem could behave in such a fashion . . ."

Lord Spenser's sudden guilty expression brought sudden insight and she kicked his other leg.

"Ow!" he bellowed. "What was *that* for?"

"You never wrote that poem," she informed him.

"I never said I did."

"You took credit for it, which was just as bad."

There was nothing Lord Spenser could say to this, so they

walked on in silence, each limping for a different reason. Finally they reached the outskirts of town and came upon a wheelwright, who assured Lord Spenser he would have his curricle looking like new by morning. No amount of bribery or high-handed behavior, however, could induce the man to guarantee its readiness before then. But there was, he assured them, a very good inn in town and he was sure they could put them up for the night. "Just go straight down this road. Can't miss it," he said cheerfully.

In her sour mood Cecily felt like kicking him, too, just for being so happy when she felt so miserable. But she refrained from doing so and followed Lord Spenser out into the late afternoon sunshine. Her kid slippers were designed for riding in carriages, not for walking the rough, rock-strewn Brighton road, and by now she was limping badly, tears of pain staining her face.

Lord Spenser looked at the sorry sight and decided to call a truce. Taking pity on her he scooped her into his arms. "You cannot walk another step," he said kindly.

"You were right. I should have ridden one of your horses," Cecily sniffed.

His lordship wisely refrained from agreeing with her, stoically marching on in silence.

As Lord Spenser carried her along, the memory of her earlier desire for adventure came back to haunt her. She remembered some of the horrid things that had happened to the heroine in a book she had just read and supposed one wasn't truly having an adventure unless something horrible happened. Horrid things were much better to read about than to experience, Cecily decided with a jagged sigh.

By the time they reached the inn Lord Spenser's horses had been led away and safely stabled, and the innkeeper was waiting with a large tankard of ale for him and cider for Cecily. Lord Spenser put her down and received the offering thankfully. Cecily, too, took hers gratefully. There may have been a time when she would have turned up her nose at having the same drink offered her wherever she went. That was a thing of the past. She drank the juice greedily and then embarrassed herself by emitting a most unladylike and unexpected belch.

His Lordship had also had a long day, and although he tried, he was unable to prevent a snicker.

Cecily had come close to feeling charitable toward Lord Spenser because he had carried her the last leg of their journey, but again his lordship fell from grace. She tossed her head and swept up the steps and into the building. His lordship followed, taking a very ungentlemanly delight in her embarrassment.

Once inside he bespoke a private parlor, and within twenty minutes he and his tired companion were sitting at a table loaded with all the good things necessary for afternoon tea. Cecily poured herself a cup and sighed. "What are we to do now?"

His lordship pulled his watch from his waistcoat. "This should bring enough to hire a chaise to take us to London," he said.

"And how shall we pay for this?" Cecily asked, gesturing to the heavily laden table.

Lord Spenser bristled. "I believe I have enough money to pay for our food."

Not taking the hint, Cecily rummaged in her reticule and fished out five one-pound notes. "Will this help?"

"There is no need," his lordship assured her, greatly insulted.

"I should like to help," said Cecily.

"It is not your fault I had not come away better prepared for a mishap," said Lord Spenser stiffly.

"No, but according to you it *is* my fault we had that mishap and I should feel better if I could help."

"Please do not fret yourself. Everything will be fine," his lordship assured her.

Cecily stuffed the notes back in her reticule and regarded her companion. He looked as tired as she felt. Mistaking her thoughtful regard for one of accusation, he rose immediately. "I shall go right now and see what I can do about getting you home," he said. "You will be perfectly safe here until I return." He then left her.

Cecily sighed and looked out the window. She wondered what time it was. It must be getting late, she thought, for the sun was riding low in the sky. How much longer before sunset? How much longer before she was home? She bit her lip in an effort not to cry. What a terrible coil. "I had much rather be on Hounslow Heath being robbed all over again," she told herself.

• 18 •

ELIZABETH SAT INSIDE her barouche nervously twisting the edge of her cloak. What a coil! That foolish child had been a spoilt little nuisance ever since she could remember. Now, after careening all over the countryside unchaperoned with Lord Spenser they would be lucky if they found anyone for her. Poor Gerald! And poor Adriana. She was bound to blame herself for this. If only the girl's mama had come to town with her instead of staying at home and nursing her imagined illnesses. . . . Ah, well, what good was it to refine upon these things now?

The carriage pulled up in front of the Wallingford townhouse and Elizabeth waited impatiently while Henry, her footman, knocked on the door. Hastings answered and she saw him shake his head. Not home! Where could she be? "I shall go in and leave a message," she informed Henry before he could speak.

Elizabeth was out of her carriage and inside the house in a flash. "Where has your mistress gone?" she asked Hastings.

"She went out for a drive with his lordship," replied the butler calmly.

Elizabeth felt like shaking him. "Hastings," she said between clenched teeth. "Where did Adriana and my brother go?"

"I am sorry to say they did not tell me," replied Hastings with detached calm.

"I shall leave a message, then," said Elizabeth.

"Very good, my lady," replied Hastings, conducting her to the library.

A hastily scrawled note to Adriana that Cecily was somewhere between London and Reigate was left and Elizabeth flew out of the house and back to her carriage. "Home—quickly!" she ordered her driver and they clattered off down the street.

Elizabeth had no better luck at her own house than she had had at her brother's. Lord Raine was not yet home, so all Elizabeth could do was dispatch their footman to White's with an urgent message that he come home immediately.

It was nearly teatime when Charles arrived and he was not happy to hear he was about to be whisked off without so much as a crumb. "I am famished, Bess, and if I am to go haring all over the countryside I will at least do so with something in my belly. We have time for a quick bite while the carriage is being made ready."

Elizabeth looked at her husband in great irritation. "How you can think about food at a time like this is more than I can fathom," she said, pulling the cord which set the little bell ringing in the servants' quarters.

"I can think about food because I am being practical." replied Raine. "I don't think well on an empty stomach."

"You do not think well on a full one, either," his wife reminded him. "It makes you sleepy."

"I have never in my life gotten full from the few crumbs that arrive on the afternoon tea tray," said Raine.

Elizabeth sat down, resigned to losing another precious hour before she could pursue her thoughtless cousin.

Her husband, however, did not dawdle over his meal. In a mere ten minutes he wolfed down five cucumber sandwiches and two tea cakes, washing them down with a quick cup of tea. He forced his wife to eat something also. "Once we are on the road," he told her, "we won't stop. And we could have a long night ahead of us."

Even though they had eaten quickly it seemed an eternity to Elizabeth before they were installed in his lordship's well-sprung carriage and rolling smoothly over the cobblestones. "Don't worry, sweetheart," he said, patting her hand. "We will find her. Spenser is a good fellow, really, and I am sure everything will turn out fine."

Elizabeth wasn't so sure, but she bit her lip and said nothing.

The servants of both families had much to say, however. At the Wallingford establishment there was much discussion of the day's events belowstairs as the servants took their meal. There had been no sign of Lord Wallingford and his lady since before teatime and there was great curiosity over what could have caused their sudden departure and why his lordship's sister was so anxious to find them. "They weren't dressed as though they were going out to dine," ventured the underbutler.

"If they were going out to dine they would have taken his lordship's carriage, not his curricle. And they certainly would not have left in the middle of the afternoon," Hastings informed him.

Mrs. Grimble shook her head. "Very odd goings on, very odd indeed."

"And we have not seen Miss Cecily all day, either," said Rosie, one of the maids.

At this statement everyone turned to look at the unfortunate Sarah, who turned beet red.

"Sarah, what do you know about this?" demanded Mrs. Grimble.

"N-nothing," stammered Sarah.

"You do too," said Rosie accusingly. "And you never told me!"

"I couldn't," said Sarah, turning to her friend. "She swore me to secrecy—told me not to tell anyone, she did."

"She's eloped!" declared Mrs. Grimble. "Oh, dearie me, our poor mistress."

"She has not eloped!" cried Sarah, ready to defend her young mistress to the death. "She only went on a curricle race to Reigate with Lord Spenser." All eyes turned to Sarah, and the kitchen table became very quiet. Sarah bit her lip and squirmed.

Rosie's eyes grew round. "With Lord Spenser?" she asked.

Sarah nodded unhappily.

Mrs. Grimble shook her head. "And not back yet. No wonder they was all in such a hurry."

"And that would explain why his lordship's sister was here," said James, the footman. He let out a low whistle.

"That will be enough," said Hastings sternly. "I am sure this is nothing his lordship cannot handle."

Later, at the Running Footman, James confided to his friend Henry Miss Cecily's latest adventure.

"So that explains why my lady was so upset," Henry said, remembering Lady Elizabeth's frantic behavior that afternoon. "She came home acting like she was being chased by three devils. She had me so scared I ran all the way to White's. They barely took time for tea and then went off in the carriage. No one knew whether to wait dinner for them or not."

"Well," said James, "I would be surprised if you don't end up with half the night off. They will most likely be busy scouring the Brighton road till at least ten."

"Most likely," agreed Henry, taking a deep drink from his mug.

"Never tell me there is trouble in the noble houses of Raine and Wallingford," said a high-pitched voice next to Henry.

Henry and James both looked coldly at their uninvited companion. "What are you doing here, Hobbs?" asked James.

"Enjoying a little time to myself, same as you. Her lazyship is not feeling up to going out tonight and is in bed with her hartshorn and biscuits. But let us not talk about me. My establishment is so boring. Tell me, just who are your interesting employers scouring the Brighton road for tonight?"

"If our employers were scouring the floor it would be no business of yours," said Henry.

"Ooh, so very high in the instep ever since her ladyship added you to her menagerie."

Henry drew back his fist to punch the offender but James stopped him. "You shouldn't want to soil your hand," he said glowering at Hobbs.

"Sticks and stones," replied Hobbs airily. "But never mind. You need not bother to tell me for I think I can piece together what has happened. Shall I demonstrate my powers of deduction to you?" His companions merely glared at him. Hobbs took this for encouragement and continued. "What, or should I say, who is so valuable that two important and busy men such as Lords Raine and Wallingford would leave the comforts of hearth and home to go looking for? Is there not a very beautiful young lady staying with Lord Wallingford—Miss Cecily Hammond, to be exact?" Henry and James exchanged concerned looks. Hobbs smiled knowingly. "Ah-huh," he said, nodding his head slowly. "Now there is a valuable jewel I should hate to lose if I were his lordship. And the Brighton road. Now, with whom could she be traveling the Brighton road? It could be any one of a number of admirers but I have heard she is showing a marked preference for Lord Spenser these days." Hobbs's eyes darted quickly to each of his companions' faces. Both showed studied indifference. A slow smile grew on Hobb's face. "Is not Gretna Green the opposite direction? Ah, well, any town will do when a man is set on deflowering a young lady."

"That's it," growled Henry, dropping his refined accent. "Ees 'ad it. I'm goin' to pop 'im one."

Hobbs was too fast and he ducked and made good his escape before Henry could shake his fist loose from James's grasp.

"What are you trying to do," hissed James, "create a scene? May as well jump up on a table and announce that Miss Cecily's disappeared to everyone here."

Henry subsided and watched the retreating figure of Hobbs. "May as well anyhow. Before the galloping mouth is through everyone in the room will know. Then he'll be on his way home to tell. And when that gossiping lady's maid at Randall house gets wind of this we've had it."

"They may find her and get back in time to put in an appearance at Almack's tonight," said James encouragingly. "Then everything will be right and tight."

Hobbs had stopped at a table near the door and was holding an animated conversation with the two men seated there and nodding in their direction.

Henry sighed. "You should have let me plant him a facer."

• 19 •

IT SEEMED TO George that he and Kate had checked at every inn and posting house between London and Croyden. No one had seen the missing couple. Dark had fallen and George was getting worried. "It seems we should have come upon them by now," he said. "In fact, we should have passed them on the road. Spenser would never bring Miss Hammond back this late. They must have met with an accident."

"Let us not think the worst," said Kate consolingly. "After all, even if they have had a mishap it could have been a small one. We might even find them on our next stop, just waiting for someone to rescue them."

Truer words were never spoken, for at the inn in Merstham Cecily and Lord Spenser sat glaring at each other across a table still laden with food although each of them had eaten every morsel from plates they had heaped high with cold ham, roast partridge, anchovies and freshly baked bread. Cecily had been toying with a tart, but pushed it away in disgust. "Not a post chaise to be had," she muttered, and again favored her companion with a sour look.

"I cannot blame the man for not wanting to rent his last carriage for anything other than pound notes," said Lord Spenser. "And I can hardly be blamed that the owner of the pawn shop had closed up early and disappeared." He took his tiepin from the table and stuck it haphazardly back in his cravat, sighing. "We have at least been able to secure seats back to London on the night coach."

"I do not relish seeing the countryside from the top of the coach," said Cecily. "In fact, I should prefer to stay here. My reputation will be ruined, but at least I shall remain in one piece."

"Everyone who rides on top of a carriage don't fall off," snapped Lord Spenser. "Anyhow, it is the only way we can get you back to London before morning so we really have no choice."

"I don't want to ride on top of a coach at night!" wailed Cecily. "It will be cold and dangerous and . . . oh, why doesn't someone find us?"

Even as Cecily was speaking help was on the way. "This is the last town before Reigate," said George as he and Kate approached Merstham. "They must be here."

"Even if they are not, do you think we might dare stop long enough for a cup of tea? I am afraid I am getting a little cold," said Kate.

"Of course," replied George. "I must say it was very kind of you to offer to come along. I am sure Cecily will be glad to see you."

"With you?" asked Kate, a smile lurking around the corners of her mouth.

"If they have run into difficulties I imagine by now she would be glad to see the devil himself," said George as they drove into town.

Once inside the inn George began his speech. "I am looking for a lady and a gentleman. The lady is about this tall. She has black hair and large violet eyes, a perfect straight nose and a beautiful mouth," George continued, warming to his subject.

"Yes!" exclaimed the innkeeper. "And the gent with her

is also very good-looking—tall, with broad shoulders and—"

"Yes," interrupted George, not wanting to hear more of his rival's attractions. "Have you seen them?"

"Most certainly I have. Got 'em in my private parlor this very moment."

George clapped his hands. "Excellent!" Before the innkeeper could say another word he rushed back outside to Kate. "I have found them," he informed her. "And we are just in time for dinner."

George ordered the groom to give his horses a good rubdown and a bag of oats and led Kate into the inn. As they approached the private parlor, good smells wafted out from the kitchen, and even more intriguing, the sound of raised voices came to them from behind the closed door.

George raised an eyebrow at Kate, who smiled and said, "It doesn't sound as if they have been wounded in any way, does it?" They heard a crash followed by the sound of shattering china. "But someone could be if we do not hurry," she added.

George cautiously opened the door and poked his head inside. "Atherby!" exclaimed Lord Spenser, a look of relief spreading across his face.

"George!" cried Cecily. She ran and threw herself into his arms. "Thank God someone has found us."

"There, there," murmured George. "Everything is all right."

"Oh, yes, now that you are here everything will be all right," Cecily said. "Lord Spenser's curricle broke down and we had to walk to town and he has spoken in a most horrid and rude manner to me. And he booked two seats home on the night coach to London and was going to make me ride on top and . . ." Cecily stopped on seeing Kate. She drew out of the circle of George's arms. "Why is Kate with you?"

"She came to help me look for you. We have all been worried about you ever since Farrell told us what happened."

"Farrell!" exclaimed Lord Spenser. "Have you seen him?"

"Yes, at Gunter's."

Before George could finish his explanation Cecily turned on Lord Spenser. "At Gunter's! You despicable man. This was all a plan to compromise me!"

"Compromise you?" squeaked Lord Spenser. "Are you mad? Madam, if I were to compromise you I should have to marry you and I'd sooner marry a harpy!"

"Ooh—I hate you!" Cecily screeched, then promptly burst into tears.

Kate put an arm around her and said to George, "I think we had best find a room where we can freshen up."

George, still in shock from the scene he had just witnessed, merely nodded.

Lord Spenser, flushed from embarrassment as well as anger, poured himself a glass of port.

"If you don't mind my asking, how many of those have you had?" said George.

"Not nearly enough," replied his lordship, running a hand through his hair. "Who would have thought such a beautiful girl could be so spoiled. And have such a temper! Do you know she kicked me? Twice!"

George smiled at this. He had seen a few glimpses of his beloved's temper. "I can believe it," he said.

Lord Spenser began to pace. "Believe me, Atherby, I have never talked like that to a female in my life. But this one—I have never met anyone so provoking! I am sorry. I know you are somehow related by marriage, and I know you are fond of the girl."

"I am," agreed George calmly.

"But really, it was too much, too much," Lord Spenser muttered, shaking his head. "I should have known better than to take a female along on a race. And by the way, what the devil happened to Farrell?"

"His sister took sick. By the time his mother got done with him he was considerably shaken and he completely forgot about you."

Lord Spenser plopped into a chair and shook his head. "And to think we thought something had happened to them."

"We were afraid you might have come to that conclusion," said George.

Lord Spenser suddenly remembered his manners. He poured George a drink and handed it to him. "I'll wager you could use this almost as much as I."

"It has been a long day," admitted George.

Lord Spenser hesitated for a moment, then cleared his throat. "Look, Atherby. About that curst poem. About all of this . . ."

George held up a hand for silence. "Let's forget it," he said. He took a sip of port, sighed tiredly and plopped into a chair.

Lord Spenser sank into a chair opposite him. "You are right, Atherby," he said. "It has been a long day."

Kate was saying the same thing to Cecily, who was already repenting her display of temper. "You were tired and upset, which made you cross. I am sure Lord Spenser understands. Or, at least he will after he has had a good night's sleep and gotten his curricle repaired. Remember, gentlemen do tend to get out of sorts when their playthings are broken."

"He was worse than out of sorts," said Cecily. "He was beastly! But, then, so was I," she admitted. "Oh, I wish I had never set out on this foolish adventure. Adriana must be so worried by now."

"No. I am sure she is not. Lady Elizabeth will have told her where you are and that we have gone to fetch you home, so I am sure all will be well."

Cecily twisted her sodden handkerchief and sighed. "You were right, you know."

"About what?" asked Kate.

"About choosing a husband," said Cecily. "And so was Adriana. She said there was more to a man than his title and fortune." Cecily looked shyly at her friend. "I suppose you and George have come to an understanding."

"Oh, we have," replied Kate agreeably.

Cecily's lower lip began to tremble. "I am sure I wish you happy," she said.

Kate smiled at her friend. "Thank you. I expect to be. Albert is such a dear."

Cecily looked at Kate blankly. "Albert?" she repeated.

"Yes," said Kate gaily. "Albert and I have become engaged."

"You have?" Cecily jumped up from the bed on which she had been sitting and hugged her friend. "That is wonderful news. And, oh, Kate, I *do* wish you happy."

Downstairs Lord Spenser was wishing the same to George, who had announced his intention of offering for Cecily, news which, after his trying afternoon, came as a great relief to Lord Spenser. Now that they were no longer rivals, they were fast on their way to becoming friends. "I know it is none of my affair, but, I say, are you absolutely sure about this, Atherby? I wish you could have been with us this afternoon. The lady does have a . . ."

"Temper," George finished in unison with Lord Spenser. "I know she does. But she is also quick to forgive. And I know she is rather spoilt. But when it comes down to it, what beauty is not?"

Lord Spenser shrugged philosophically and nodded. "True. And I will say this for her. She is pluck to the backbone. You should have seen her coming out of London. Not so much as one entreaty to slow down." Lord Spenser picked up the bottle of port and refilled George's glass. "Let me be the first to wish you well." He raised his glass to George. "To your happiness."

"His happiness, eh?"

The two men turned to see an angry-looking Albert standing in the open door. He hurled his hat and gloves at a nearby chair. "He will never live to enjoy it for I am going to tear his black heart out of his body!" And with that Albert rushed at George, hands going for his throat.

"What are you doing?" spluttered George angrily as Albert grabbed him by the throat and pulled him from his chair.

"You traitor!" bellowed Albert, trying to shake George and keep the stranglehold on his throat at the same time.

"Have you gone mad, Eagan?" cried Lord Spenser. "Let go, man, you're choking him!"

This did not seem to bother Albert at all. If anything, his grip on George's throat tightened.

Lord Spenser jumped into the fray, and all three men went crashing around the room, knocking food from the table and tipping over chairs. A gooseberry tart tumbled to the ground and George put his heel in it. His foot skated out from under him and he fell backward, taking the other two men with him. They landed on the floor in a writhing, grunting heap.

"George! Albert! What are you doing," cried Cecily from the doorway. "Oh, stop this at once, do!" She turned to Kate, who was standing next to her with a horrified look on her face. "We must stop them."

"Albert!" cried Kate, rushing into the room. "Stop this madness at once!"

Lord Spenser finally managed to pull an angry, panting Albert away from George and the two young men got up and stood glaring at each other. "I say, Eagan, what is this about?" his lordship demanded.

"This is about stealing a friend's betrothed from right under his nose," panted Albert.

"You were engaged to Miss Hammond?" asked the confused Lord Spenser incredulously.

"Miss Hammond? What are you talking about? I was engaged to Miss Courtland. And this villain ran off with her," Albert accused.

"Albert," said Kate, "didn't Mr. Farrell tell you?"

"Yes, and I must say I call it a shabby thing to do. And to think it was I who put up your name for membership at Brooks's. Wait a minute," said Albert, stopping himself in the middle of his tirade. "What are you doing here, Spenser? And . . . Miss Hammond?" Albert scratched his head.

"They are here quite by accident," explained Kate. "And it is because of them that we are here. We came looking for them. Mr. Farrell was to find you and tell you where we had gone and why."

"You mean you are not running off with Atherby?" asked Albert.

"Oh, Albert, how could you think such a thing of us," said Kate.

Albert blushed and hung his head.

"Is this a private party or may we join you?" a deep voice asked from the doorway.

Cecily gulped. "Cousin Gerald!"

"Hello, Cecily. Ah, I see you have ordered dinner," Wallingford said to Lord Spenser. "But this will never be enough. Perhaps you would be so good as to see what else the innkeeper has in his larder, for I am quite famished, and I believe my wife is, also."

He disappeared and returned a few moments later with Adriana. At the sight of her Cecily turned white and stumbled back into the nearest chair. "Hello everyone," said Adriana brightly. "Lord Spenser, what a delightful idea to have this impromptu little dinner."

"Why, yes," agreed Kate, catching on. "Isn't it a pity Mr. Farrell and his sister could not make it. It would have been such a lovely surprise for them. They will be disappointed when they hear what a fine evening they missed."

Lord Spenser looked around at his chattering, unexpected dinner guests and scratched his head.

Wallingford, seeing his puzzled expression, took him aside and said, "It is getting rather late, and as you know, the kind of unexpected turn of events which you appear to have experienced today can often be misunderstood. This will possibly save both you and my cousin, er, considerable embarrassment."

Understanding dawned on Lord Spenser and he grabbed Wallingford's hand and shook it fervently. "Oh, yes. Thank you. *Thank* you."

Wallingford smiled. "I somehow thought you would thank me."

Lord Spenser flushed. "Your niece is a very beautiful girl—pluck to the backbone. But, that is . . ."

Lord Wallingford lifted a silencing hand. "You would not suit. I feel the same. Of course, I realize none of this is of your making. We have picked up bits of your story along the way, and the innkeeper here was able to fill in the last missing pieces of the puzzle for me. I suspect you have had quite a time of it."

Lord Spenser let out a sigh of relief and, thinking of his sore shins, again thanked Wallingford for being so understanding.

The chairs were righted, the covers laid and the table was again piled high with food, which the hungry travelers eagerly fell upon. Midway through the meal their number was again increased as an amazed Lord Raine and his lady entered the room. Unperturbed, Wallingford saluted his sister and brother-in-law with his fork. "Charles, Elizabeth! Come in. I had no idea Spenser had invited you to his dinner party, also. The food here is excellent, you know."

• 20 •

LORD SPENSER'S IMPROMPTU party was a merry one. George related Lord Farrell's description of his trials with a sick sister and an upset mama and even Cecily, who had been rather subdued all evening, smiled.

After an hour the guests felt refreshed enough to make the trip back to town and began to collect wraps and pull on gloves. Lord Spenser elected to stay the night in Merstham and wait for his curricle to be repaired. George promised to send his valet to him, feeling it was the least he could do for his new friend.

"I am truly sorry for all the trouble I caused you," Cecily told him penitently as the group made their way out the door. "I hope you will forgive me."

"Only if you promise to forget all the ungentlemanly things I said," replied Lord Spenser, taking her hand.

Cecily smiled at him. "The first part of our adventure was wonderful and I shall always remember that," she said.

With the exception of Kate, who preferred to ride home with Albert, the ladies were bundled into Lord Raine's spacious carriage, their legs covered with rugs to keep away the chill of the spring night. The gentlemen climbed up onto the curricles and with waves and good wishes all left Lord Spenser standing in the doorway of the inn, looking very much the part of the amiable host. He waved at the departing company then sauntered back inside to finish the last of a half-empty bottle of port.

Inside Lord Raine's carriage there was little conversation. Adriana stopped Cecily midway through a tearful apology. "Let us not talk of it, love. You are safe and that is all that matters to me. Surely a curricle race cannot be much worse than staging a robbery," she added and squeezed Cecily's hand.

Cecily returned the squeeze and, with a jagged sigh, laid her head back against the squabs and shut her eyes. Before they had gone five miles the dark interior of the carriage was filled with the sound of gentle snores.

Wallingford and his ladies arrived home late that night, but no later than if they had been to a ball, and after her nap in the carriage Adriana felt much refreshed and able to cope with dropping hints to satisfy the unasked questions of the servants. She saw Cecily safely bundled off to bed and then joined her lord, who was sitting in the library enjoying the fire and a glass of brandy. "It has been quite a day," she said, leaning down to put her arms around him.

"Yes," replied his lordship. "It certainly did prove interesting. Promise me, love, we shall have only boys. They are much less worry than females," he said, drawing his wife onto his lap.

Adriana laughed. "I must say I agree with you," she said. She shook her head. "Poor Lord Spenser. He did have quite a day, did he not?"

"That he did. But by now I am sure he feels no pain—and won't until tomorrow morning when he awakes with a splitting head and gets the bill from the wheelwright, who will most likely gouge him. But he is getting off cheaply. Just think, if our merry little party had not come along he would most likely have had to marry Cecily."

Adriana chuckled. "It looks as if we have managed to

successfully scotch a scandal. And I am so glad. Do you think George has a chance with Cecily now?"

"He may," admitted Wallingford with a tired sigh.

"Oh, you are bone tired," said Adriana, pushing a stray lock from his forehead. "I think we can safely retire. Cecily is back. We have outsmarted the gossips. All is well with the world."

But all was not as well as Adriana thought. Hobbs had been busy that night. He had only paused at the Running Footman long enough to spread the story of Miss Hammond's disappearance to a small handful of his cronies. Then he had hurried back to Randall house where he promptly shared the news with the underbutler and Lady Randall's hairdresser. The next morning while she was doing Lady Randall's hair the extremely fast behavior of Miss Cecily Hammond was repeated in as much detail as one who had none of the facts at her disposal could do.

"I always considered Wallingford's bride a flighty thing—certainly too young to supervise a girl's come out," snorted Lady Randall. "I must say it serves Genevieve Hammond right for being so lazy as to trust someone else with her daughter's future."

When Lady Cecil came to pay a morning call on Lady Randall later that day she heartily agreed. "These spoiled young beauties start their Season with much too good an opinion of themselves and think they may get away with anything."

"Well, she *is* Wallingford's cousin," said Lady Randall.

"Nonetheless," replied Lady Cecil, "if this rumor is accurate, which we must assume it is, as I saw not one of them at Almack's last night, such fast behavior should not be tolerated."

"Yes, you are right, Amelia," agreed Lady Randall.

* * *

Cecily slept late and awoke to a beautiful day. The sun was out and at Wallingford House there was no hint of the storm clouds gathering over her head. She spent her afternoon in happy anticipation of the ball she was to attend that night. Many young men had already solicited her hand for a dance and she knew, before the evening had barely begun, that all of her dances would be spoken for. But she would save a waltz for George. It was the least she could do for the man who had spent the better part of the previous day looking for her. A vision of George in the doorway of the inn at Merstham came to mind and she smiled. She would save him another dance as well.

George also spent his afternoon in blissful ignorance of the social peril surrounding his beloved. He had awoke with hope in his heart and bounded out of bed with a spring in his step. Lord Spenser, his most serious rival for Cecily's affection, was now out of the running. And Cecily had looked so glad to see him the night before—surely a good sign. Knowing he would be attending the same ball as Cecily that night, he set out for the nearest flower shop and ordered violets to be sent to Cecily. Then, since he was already out, he spent some time just sauntering along Bond Street, enjoying the pleasant amusement of seeing and being seen. He bought some snuff from Messrs. Fribourg and Treyer, then went to Rundell and Bridge, where he bought a new snuffbox. And to make sure he would properly impress Cecily, he purchased some new Belcher handkerchiefs, a new cravat, and some Russian oil with which to pomade his locks. Finally tired of spending what little was left of his money, George wandered in the general direction of home, stopping first at Tattersall's to place a bet and then going round by Albert's lodgings in Ryder Street. George was disappointed to find his friend gone from home, as he had been hoping to show him his new purchases and pass the time. Albert was probably out with Kate and enjoying having her all to himself, thought George with a smile.

But Albert was not out with Kate. Albert was at George's lodgings, pacing the floor and looking out the window. When George finally reached his doorstep, it was Albert who opened the door and pulled him in. "Where the devil have you been?" he demanded.

George looked at his friend and blinked. "I was out. I purchased a new snuffbox. Would you like to see it?"

"No, I would not," snapped Albert. "Good heavens, man. Can't you see something has happened?"

George stared at Albert and dropped into the nearest chair. "What do you mean? What has happened?"

"Miss Hammond's reputation has been ruined. That is what has happened," said Albert.

"What?" squeaked George. "How can that be?"

Albert shook his head. "Don't know. The servants talked, most likely."

"Are you sure about this?"

"Of course I'm sure. I came here straight from Kate's. I can tell you, this whole thing has made Kate's mama and papa anything but happy. Her mama gave me a regular bear garden jaw last night when I brought her home. Made me promise to send the announcement for our engagement to the *Gazette* first thing this morning. I wanted to send it weeks ago and said so, but nobody listened," Albert finished in aggrieved tones.

"Yes, well, I don't see how that could cause Cecily to be . . ." George began.

"There's more," said Albert. "I returned this afternoon to take Kate driving and found her and her mama both upset. Kate's mama don't want Kate to even so much as give Miss

Hammond the nod when she sees her on the street. Stories about her and Spenser are flying all over town. There's even a rumor that they spent the night together in Reigate."

George's mouth flew open. "Why, that's a damned lie!"

"Of course it is," agreed Albert. "But you know what happens when the gossips get started."

George suddenly felt very helpless. How did one fight gossip? "What can I do?" he asked.

"I don't know, but you'd better think of something," said Albert.

George spent the remaining hours before the ball trying to think of something but could come up with no brilliant solution to Cecily's problem. He only knew he had to be at that ball to dance with Cecily and tell her silly things to make her laugh. He would make sure she never even noticed the thinning in the ranks of suitors or the snubs of the ignorant and uninformed.

George took special care over his toilet that evening. He was generous with the Russian oil and took even more pains than usual when tying his cravat. Finally, after one last careful inspection in his looking glass, George pronounced himself satisfied with what he saw and set off for Grosvenor Square. He could have taken a chair, but George knew he needed the walk to rid himself of some of his nervous energy. He strode purposefully along the streets he had come to know so well the past few weeks, oblivious to all around him, his thoughts centered on Cecily and his senses dulled. He never heard the shuffling of feet behind him when he passed the dark alleyway. He barely had time for a startled cry when rough hands grabbed him, ripping his coat. He felt a sudden, stabbing pain at the back of his head and saw the starlit sky no longer high above him but spread out across the back of his eyelids. He fell to the ground with a moan.

George awoke with a throbbing head. He lay on his back and on opening his eyes was relieved to see that the stars were once again where they belonged. He tried to sit up but his spinning head and queasy stomach warned him against it and he lay back down on the dirty cobblestones. How long had he been out? What time was it? He reached for his watch and found his waistcoat pocket empty. "Curst foot-pads," he growled. He studied the sky. There was as yet no sign of dawn. Perhaps he hadn't been unconscious long. He made another effort to sit up and this time succeeded. Holding his head, he staggered to his feet and leaned against the nearest wall, surveying his ruined evening clothes. There was no help for it. He would have to return home and change. He could never gain admittance to a ball looking like this. A change of wardrobe, some wine, and he would be fine. And when he set out again he would take a chair. He could only hope the night was not too far gone and that the ball wouldn't be ending by the time he got there. Step by step, he began to inch his way back the direction he had come. Cecily, his mind chanted. Cecily! He must help Cecily. He must . . . George tripped and fell to the ground. His head was splitting. He put both hands against the back of his head in the hopes that the pain would go away and shut his eyes.

• 21 •

LORD WALLINGFORD AND his ladies arrived at the ball fashionably late and the festivities were already under way. But their host and hostess were still greeting arriving guests and there seemed to be no end to the ever growing line of arrivals that stretched by them and on to the ballroom. As they filed slowly along, waiting their turn to greet their hostess, Cecily noticed some rather odd looks coming from some of the older ladies in line. "Is there anything amiss with my gown or hair?" she whispered to Adriana, wondering if the violets George had sent clashed with her gown.

Adriana studied her carefully and could find no discernable rip or tear in the pale pink, high-waisted gown. "I can see nothing amiss," she said. "In fact, you look charming. Why do you ask?"

"Because Lady Cecil and Lady Ann Downey just gave me the oddest look. And when I smiled at them they pretended they had not seen me and looked the other way."

Adriana's eyes widened in dismay.

"What is it?" asked Cecily, her heart sinking at the expression on Adriana's face. "What is wrong."

"Never mind, love," said Adriana. She was silent a moment, then touched Cecily's arm and whispered, "If anyone should ask you about your movements yesterday just say several of us raced to Reigate and then dined in Merstham as Lord Spenser's guests."

Cecily looked in panic at Adriana. "Do you think people mean to cut me?"

"Don't worry, love. We shall ride this out. But you must put on a brave face. Try to appear as merry as possible no matter what happens," Adriana replied under her breath. "Lilleth," she cried, turning to her hostess. "This promises to be a real crush. I congratulate you."

"Thank you," replied her good friend. Pulling her close for a kiss the lady whispered, "There are some nasty rumors flying around. What can I do to help you?"

"Ask me how I enjoyed my race to Reigate," Adriana whispered back.

"And how did you enjoy your race to Reigate?" asked her friend.

"It was delightful," Adriana replied gaily. "Lord Spenser quite beat us all and we had the merriest supper party in Merstham on the way home."

The two dowagers hovering near the entrance to the ballroom looked put out.

Adriana sailed on by them. "Good evening, Lady Cecil," Adriana said airily. And with sudden concern she asked, "You are not feeling ill, are you?"

Lady Cecil bristled at this impertinence. "No. I am not."

"Oh. You did not look well for a moment. One must be so careful these days not to take poisons into their system, you know. Come, Cecily," she said and swept on.

"Impertinent minx," muttered Lady Cecil.

Lady Randall's grandson lit up at the sight of Cecily as she entered the room, a reaction not lost on his grandmother. "Harold. Remember what I told you. If you go near that fast young lady tonight I shall send for my solicitor tomorrow."

The young man sighed. "Yes, Grandmother."

Few of Cecily's admirers came near her. Even Sir Winston seemed to have lost interest and was paying court to, of all people, Lady Penelope, who smiled condescendingly at Cecily from across the room. The beautiful Miss Hammond danced her first dance with her cousin. The faithful Albert solicited her hand for a set of country dances, but after that Cecily found herself sitting in one of the dainty chairs placed up against the wall, one of the season's most beautiful wallflowers.

This was not lost on Adriana and the light of battle came into her eyes. Seeing Mr. Farrell and his mama on the far end of the room she quickly made her way to them. She made her curtsy to Mr. Farrell's mama and inquired after Miss Farrell's health. "I was so sorry to hear you had taken ill and were unable to finish the race," she said. "Lord Spenser had invited a number of us to Reigate to share the adventure and we were naturally very concerned when you did not show up."

"But I did not know anyone else—" began Mr. Farrell.

"My dear sir, did you think I knew nothing about this?" interrupted Adriana. She laughed. "I may be shatterbrained at times, but I assure you I knew of and was a participant in this outing. You certainly do not think I would allow my husband's cousin to go about the countryside alone with a gentleman, do you?"

Mr. Farrell admitted he had not given the matter much thought. By his mama's blush it was plain to see she had.

There, thought Adriana, moving on. At least one leak in the dike is plugged. Her eyes scanned the ballroom. There was no sign of Lord Spenser. Pity. It would have helped if he had come. For all Adriana knew he could still be lounging about Merstham in happy ignorance of the danger

Cecily was in. And where was George? Why hadn't he shown up yet? Surely he would be coming. He must!

On her way back to Cecily, Adriana saw Kate talking with two other young ladies. "Good evening, Miss Courtland," said Adriana brightly.

Kate blushed and returned the greeting. Excusing herself she walked a little apart from her companions. "How is Cecily holding up?" she whispered.

"You can see for yourself," replied Adriana. "She would be glad to talk with you."

Kate blushed again. "I shall try. I have already sent Albert to dance with her. But the truth is, Mama and Papa were not happy about yesterday's turn of events. And even though Albert and I explained everything, they are not pleased with my involvement—especially with all the rumors flying 'round. They have ordered me to stay away from her. Perhaps if you were to talk to Mama."

Adriana followed Kate's gaze to the forceful-looking matron sitting in a chair across the room. She was watching them with obvious displeasure. Adriana gulped.

Kate patted her arm. "I know," she said. "Mama can look very fierce sometimes. But she really is a love."

"Yes, I know," said Adriana.

Kate sighed. "I am sure she will come round in a few days. But for tonight, well, perhaps it would be best to . . ." Kate broke off and bit her lip. "Oh, Lady Wallingford. I do so want to help. What am I to do? I am in nearly as much trouble as Cecily."

"I know. And you have helped just by encouraging Albert to dance with her."

"I shall send him to her again before the evening is over," Kate promised. "And I shall speak to her, too–when Mama is not looking."

While Adriana fought the battle on the sidelines, Cecily's

male relations did what they could on the dance floor. Wallingford danced with her again then turned her over to his brother-in-law. Lord Raine danced with her and deposited her next to her cousin, where she now sat, pretending to enjoy herself while Elizabeth chatted with her, trying to help her maintain the façade of idle unconcern. Cecily's eyes were very bright and her smile a small one, but not a tear was allowed to escape. "I am ruined, am I not?" she finally whispered to Elizabeth.

"No. You are not," Elizabeth replied firmly. "Have you not seen Adriana flitting from person to person? She is describing a very merry dinner party in which we all participated last night. Smile."

Cecily smiled and a jagged sigh escaped her lips. She was no less beautiful than when she had first taken the ton by storm. But where were all her suitors now? Not one of them cared enough to stand by her side. Not even George. She studied the tip of her slipper and murmured, "Everyone is staring at me. I want to go home."

"You cannot," said Elizabeth in a whisper. "That will only give credibility to the rumors and then you shall truly be in trouble. You must be brave."

Cecily sniffed and blinked hard. Suddenly two elegantly shod feet connected to two skinny shanks came within her field of vision. There was only one person to whom those legs could belong. She raised her eyes hopefully.

"May I have this dance?" asked George. "I have gotten considerable practice these past weeks and I am sure I will not tread on your toes . . . or your gown."

"I believe I would not mind if you did," said Cecily shakily, rising.

George's arm circled her waist and he drew her across the dance floor in three-quarter time.

"Why are you dancing with me?" asked Cecily.

"Because I am fond of the waltz," replied George.

"There are any number of more socially acceptable ladies with whom you might dance it," Cecily pointed out.

"Yes, but I am not fond of them."

"You are dancing with me right now to save me from scandal, aren't you?" asked Cecily in a small voice.

"If you like to think that you may. I think I am dancing with you because I am very much in love with you. I suppose it all boils down to the same thing."

Cecily bit her lip and blinked hard, but this time there was no stopping the tears from escaping. And she didn't care. "I am *so* glad you are here," she said with a tiny sob. "I began to think you would not come tonight."

"I almost didn't," admitted George. "I was set upon by footpads and had to go home and change. My head hurts like the devil."

Cecily's eyes widened. "They hit you on the head?"

George nodded and winced at the pain.

"And you came anyway?"

"I wanted to help you. I heard there had been some gossip."

Cecily looked incredulous. "And you were not afraid to be seen dancing with me?"

"Why should I be afraid to be seen dancing with you?" George replied tenderly.

"What a truly brave man you are, to be sure," said Cecily.

George blushed and smiled down at her. Her eyes shone with admiration. It was a new look. One with which she had never before favored him. His smile widened.

"If you are not afraid to be seen dancing with me perhaps you will not be afraid to be seen taking me in to supper," she said shyly.

"I also might very much like to be seen riding with you in Hyde Park tomorrow," said George.

Cecily smiled at him. "I should like that," she said simply.

Adriana nodded in George and Cecily's direction as her husband swept her out onto the dance floor. "Did I not tell you he would win her in the end?"

"Yes, I suppose you did," said Wallingford. "And it looks as if you were right, love." He shook his head. "Poor George."